Long ago, when the powers of good and evil were younger than now...

TRAVELS IN NHEARN

-PART I-

-GUILT-

A STORY IN THE WORLD CREATED BY

Jared S DuBose

Travels in Nhearn: Guilt

ISBN: 979-8-218-25187-1

Discover more at:
travelsinnhearn.com

Dedicated to my grandmother
who gave me my passion for writing

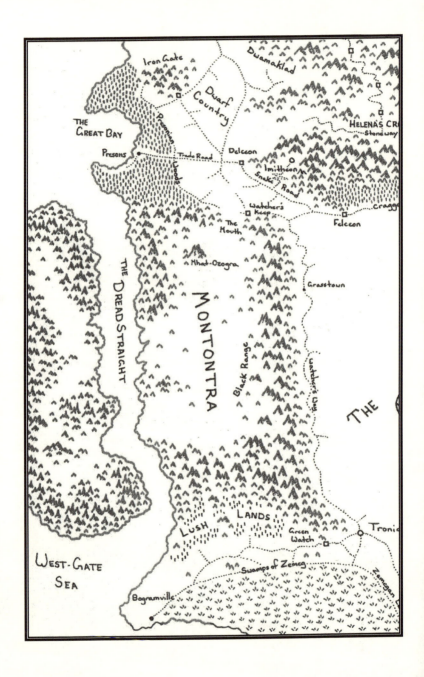

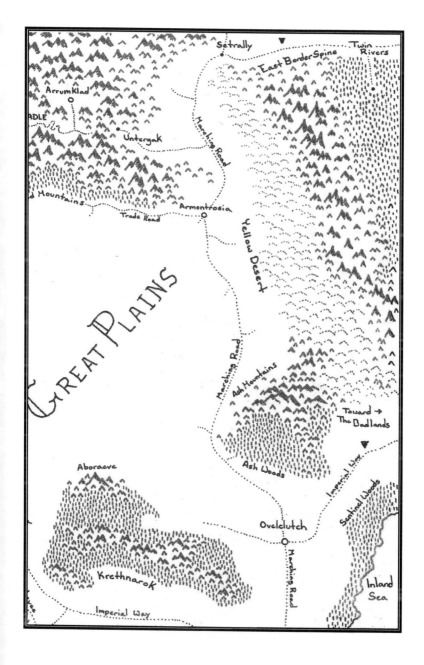

-CONTENTS-

PROLOGUE:
THE CREATION

In the beginning of all things there were four great powers that existed within the Expanse. Greatest among them was Geabythol, the Dark, who was vast and eternal. This Power was so infinite that it existed as though it were a domain unto itself. Even where it did not yet exist was a shadow so great that Geobythol's very gloom may linger still.

Allied to the great power of Darkness in eternity was a much younger power that had corrupted itself through its own great hunt. This Power was named Gedreathmogg, Death, and it was in constant pursuit of souls to satisfy a hollow hunger.

Hiding within the Darkness was Istalebreth, Life, the Crafter of Souls. With its power it was able to create wonders beyond measure, beauties indescribable, creatures incomprehensible, and things that were altogether fantastical. Where it dwelt was inevitably followed by Gedreathmogg, and Death devoured all things that Life created.

While Istalebreth fled endlessly through the Expanse, the eternal pursuit of Gedreathmogg driving it through the Dark, it eventually found a place that had been overlooked and forgotten by Geabythol. Within a great cave was a new Power that called out to

Istalebreth. It was the youngest of the four great Powers, an ally that was able to banish the Shadow within its lair, and it made itself known to Life as Istilicrel, Light.

It was in this place where Light held absolute dominion that Life was safe. Istalebreth created more than it ever had and in more amazing ways than it ever had, braver here than in the Dark. For untold eons they stayed in this forgotten place, ever watched by Death who was afraid to leave from the shadow of Geabythol and enter the illuminated cave of Istilicrel.

Darkness was told through the whispers of Death about Its enemy, the Light. Istilicrel was a taint within Geabythol's own self and a fracture that could unravel the whole of its dominion. Geabythol came upon the cave with all malice and hate that it could muster from the infinite of the Expanse. Istilicrel then defeated all that was ever known and the Expanse was only ever the Gloom of Shadow, for never again was everything watched by the Dark.

From the remains of Geabythol came Annabel, a being of Evil, who kept all the infinite malice and darkness that Geabythol had died with. Annabel continued the assault into the cave and succeeded where Geabythol could not. With her own hands she smothered the light so that upon her flesh were scars of the eternal darkness from her deed.

Light had been vanquished. From the remains of Istilicrel came Christianna, a being of Good, who kept all the duty and love that Light had felt toward Life. Opposed to Annabel, Christianna held her hands out against the evil and continued to defend Istalebreth as well as all of Life's creations.

The Power of Life was estranged from the new beings, unable to protect its purpose without the defenses of Christianna's goodness. With all the effort Istalebreth could muster, the great power engulfed upon itself and in its ultimate passing rose forth Ænoen, who took great responsibility as all of Istalebreth's power faded into the eternal Shadow. Ænoen was blessed with the purpose and freedom to create as the great power of Life had done before him.

Gedreathmog witnessed the new beings, their struggle against one another, and it prepared itself as an anchor throughout the expanse. From this foundation a great Tower emerged that was overseen by the spirit of death, Dermolgmar, who held loyalty in law and ensured that the souls of its ancient enemy were brought to the Tower and cared for in rest.

It was in this time of struggle that Ænoen found himself most powerful amongst the new beings. He created a great beacon of light, claiming it then to be Sol, center of all the realms to come, and around it Ænoen used the powers of creation to summon forth new Avatars of great purpose. Helena, Katrina, Morganna, and Anastasia, the Elemental Gods, forces of creation with design by Ænoen, now lived, and in their domains they flourished. Their realms were filled with their own imaginings and each of their domains were then brought together beside Ænoen's Sol. Each of the four elemental realms resided beside one another and met at the center of Ænoen's own domain as He intended.

Above the four realms and Ænoen's domain was the dominion of Christianna, who was given the Heavens. From her domain she could see below, through all the realms, and peer upon all that was with gladness. Below the four realms and beneath the light of Sol was taken by Annabel and she dominated any who fell to that place with malice and hate. She named her own realm, a scorn to Ænoen, and its name was whispered on the tongues of all who came to fear it. In all languages, through all of time, it was known by Ænoen, and by all others, as Hell.

Ænoen ensured that His domain was made as the most center to all the realms and that the heart of it was Sol. There He gathered an orb of love, created for it the foundations, and set it to rest beside Sol where it could bask in the light of His own heart.

When at last the creation of His love was ready He invited Helena, the Goddess of the Earth, to come from her realm to do as she willed in good faith upon the foundations. To the world she gave the mountains and carved the ravines so that at the horizon was the rise and fall of her will. When at last the peaks were risen and the canyons were sculpted, Ænoen invited Anastasia, the Goddess of the Waters, to come from her realm to do as she willed in good faith upon the foundations. To the world she gave the streams and the seas, the pools and the springs, so that every wave and trickle was the desire of her will. When at last the seas were filled and the lakes were placid, Ænoen invited Katrina, the Goddess of the Air, to come from her realm to do as she willed in good faith upon the foundations. To the world she gave the wind, and with it she swept up the waters that caused the storms, that brought the rain, that went over the mountains, that united the elements together, so that they might all be pleasurable to the world, as was her will.

As the other Gods were invited and the foundation was molded with their gifts, Annabel crept from the dark depths of Hell to speak with the final Elemental. She whispered into the ear of the Goddess of Fire to invoke a jealous rage, forcing her to witness the glee of all the

4

other Gods as their manifestations graced the new world, and forced her to see the attention that Ænoen bestowed upon the others before she was beckoned.

When the clouds had parted and the thunder diminished, Ænoen invited Morganna, the Goddess of Fire, to come from her realm to do as she willed in good faith upon the foundations. To the world she gave calamity and instead of coming in gladness she came with strife. She boiled the lakes into deserts, scarred the land into obsidian, and from the peaks of great mountains rose smoke to choke the clouds in the sky.

The terror that came made Morganna a foul name to utter and the other Elementals began to call her the Goddess of Chaos. She was met by the other three Elementals who were so ashamed for the part their sister had played that they aligned themselves and made an effort to fight Fire back into its own domain. In the mountains a blanket sheet of ice was laid down to hinder the bursting of volcanoes, and their fight was shown in great craters of dormant rock. Waters rose in massive waves along the coast where the flumes of lava met the sea and their fight was shown in great walls of steam. Where fire and ember rose into the sky great winds blew to cast out the vile fumes and their fight was shown in great barriers of smoke. With this effort they could not banish Morganna in her entirety, Ænoen's invitation a lasting thread between the realms and even still He knew her balance was needed to create His world wholly.

At last Ænoen put them all to rest, not to banishment or for punishment, but back to their rightful places so that they may watch His own domain continue to grow. Helena returned to the Realm of Earth, Anastasia to the Realm of Water, Katrina to the Realm of Air, and Morganna to the Realm of Fire. The four

Elemental Realms surrounded Ænoen's domain and they moved in orbit across his Realm together. Above them all was Heaven, below them all was Hell, and together was the universe where at its center was Ænoen's heart, Sol, with the new world they all had made beside it.

Ænoen then gathered from His mind an orb of pure thought, and He set it to rest beside His world as the world rested beside His own heart. The new foundation He left untouched by the hands of any other and He called it the Moon. From Sol was the golden light of Ænoen's love and from the Moon was the silver light of Ænoen's purpose. To guide the Moon He used the powers of creation to summon forth Aurora, the Goddess of Righteousness, and He asked that she watch always over this place they all had made. To the world she offered her judgment and she kept the powers of good and all the powers of evil in line with Ænoen's balance.

Ænoen most desired then to heal the scars that were left upon His world and He used His powers of creation to summon forth Vanessa, Goddess of Nature. Ænoen invited her from her realm of the Fey Wilde, to do as she desired in good faith upon the foundations. To the world she brought strangeness and new. Grass and flower now grew in great number where once was rock. Where once was barren now was tree. Where once was terror now was beautiful curiosity.

With the initiative of a predator and the love of a mother, Vanessa then moved about the world to meet with her sisters. She first climbed the summits where Helena could speak with her. She told the Earth, "To you, sister, I offer the winter and the evergreens who might share your heights. Your places, no matter their summits, will host such sights that the mountains will be

6

thanked for their graces and you will know my love. At your greatest peaks my trees will wither to rest underneath such heights so that these tall places can be grand and seen even below my canopy, so that you too will be loved and revered." Helena agreed and took the gift of winter to her.

Vanessa then moved to the canyons where the wind was harsh and she could hear the whispers of Katrina upon them. "To you, sister, I offer the spring and blooms of all things. Your passings will be filled with jubilance and an aroma so pleasant that the winds will be thanked for their graces and you will know my love. Upon the grass and in the trees I shall create dance and songs in your stirrings so that you too will be loved and revered." Katrina agreed and took the gift of spring to her.

Vanessa then moved to the shore where the crashing of waves was as the soft voice of Anastasia. "To you, sister, I offer the summer and the shade of full trees. There will be nothing more pleasant than your coasts and your banks beneath my canopy so that you will know my love. Within the rolling waves and nearby the babbling brooks I will honor your peace and respite with delicious vegetations so that you too will be loved and revered." Anastasia agreed and took the gift of summer to her.

Vanessa then moved to the mount of fire where few had dared since the outrage, but she was not afraid. The boiling of the earth forged the harshness of Morganna's voice yet Vanessa still spoke softly and with love to the Goddess of Chaos. "To you sister, I offer the autumn and the changing of the guard. The trees themselves will share your colors so that the light of Sol will make them as bright as fire without your hands to scar, and you will be remembered so that you will know my love. You will have the last of the year's heat to bask in so that you can see the coming of the cold so that you will slumber with peace and you will be revered in your time." Morganna, though she was cast away and felt unloved by her sister elements, took Vanessa's gift and was pleased that the autumn was hers.

She then went to Ænoen to share what she had done, and though the feud may linger, there was now unity among them. When her gifts were received and the year was in balance Vanessa returned to the Fey Realm but left her heart in the woodlands of the world, for she loved them more at times than her own domain. Ænoen knew and allowed for it. He let her come and go as she pleased so long as she created beauty and healed the scars to come.

In its creation Ænoen took great pride. The firmament of His love He now named Nhearn, and all the gods would come to call the world Nhearn as He proclaimed it to be. In this place rose the waves, to break them rose the mountains, to break them rose the storms, to balance them rose the molten earth, and to heal all to pass was wild change.

After the foundation of Nhearn stood against the void, Ænoen was rendered tired and He walked along the shores of His creation. Dark it was among the Expanse where the Shadow still lingered. Ænoen lifted a lantern of gold and from within came the light of Sol. He took His lantern from the eastern horizon and walked across the whole of Nhearn where He set it upon the western horizon. "Come daughter of the Heavens, come daughter of gold, come and find a home in this place I have made." From the golden light came Christianna who was fair and spectacular.

Ænoen then lifted a lantern of silver and from within came the light of the Moon. He took His lantern from the southern horizon and walked across the whole of Nhearn where He set it upon the very edge of the land. "Come watcher of the world, come daughter of silver, come and find a home in this place I have made." From the silver light came Aurora who was powerful and awesome.

Together they all went to witness the great work that had been done and they all were swayed by its beauty. The world of Nhearn was now the center most place to all the hearts of the Gods, all save one. As the Moon left the sky in its orbit and the light of Sol faded away into night they witnessed that Ænoen's lanterns had diminished. Darkness came and from within its terror came forth Annabel of her own uninvited devices.

Ænoen stepped forth to meet the intruder, unafraid and undaunted. "Annabel, you being so dark and arriving with such malice have shivered me. I wish that you had come in grace and by my request. You offer no light or beauty in Nhearn and where you tread is but waste and void. If you come here without any gladness and without any love then you shall fail here within my domain."

Annabel raised her hands and into the night rose a dark orb from the horizon in the south. "Behold, it is the Moon. I have spoiled it and with it the dominion of the protector. In this time you shall discover my work too late and by the cover of darkness you shall not find me until my deeds reveal themselves."

CHAPTER I
BASSAR'S PATROL

The cold Autumn air blew down from the Ash Mountains and the colorful leaves of Ash Wood rustled together in the breeze. Christof, a deputy for only the season, still a novice of the guard practice, pulled his scarf tighter and tucked a hand beneath his tunic to get his fingers warm. He leaned on his spear and with what dexterity his hands allowed he brought a pipe to his mouth with the other hand.

"A break already?"

"Aye, captain, but I mean no offense of it." Christof decided to snuff the pipe but a shake of his leader's hand allowed for the respite. "Thank you, Bassar."

"I must remember to tend to myself too. I am not young anymore." Bassar smirked, "As my daughter reminds me often enough."

"I'm still able," Christof laughed into a deep cough.

"Tell me again, what was it that you did before coming to Kurrum?"

"Retired from the Imperial Legion," Christof recovered and returned to his pipe before speaking through the smoke. "Ranger out near Green Watch in the Lush Lands west of Tronia. Got into a fair amount of trouble with orc out that way. Fire Clan orc too, big armored brutes that come from Montontra north from there, down the Dread Straight I'd wager. Had to take some of their forts head on as a special operative back then."

"Even an old soldier is good company out here in the frontier, better perhaps than the young ones. They can outpace us-"

"Eh, we know the shortcuts though," the deputy winked. "What about you, captain? You haven't been in Kurrum forever. I know your gaunt, soldier."

Bassar smiled but it quickly faded. "I have some experience," he said quietly with a suddenly serious tone. "Best be off though. The rest of the border won't watch itself."

After a moment the halt ended and the two wandered southward again. Christof used his spear as a walking stick while Bassar led on, using trails at times, but often they surveyed through the woods that were not difficult to tread upon except for the soft earth collapsing beneath the seasons shedding of leaves. "What about your lad, captain? He couldn't be one of those greenhorns you were speaking of," Christof waited to hear from Bassar for a long pause and became worried that he might have offended the captain for continuing their talk.

Relief came as Bassar caught his thoughts and spoke, "I am sure he is able, though I worry he may have too much to prove."

"Captain's son. He has some heavy boots to fill."

"I've tried taking him hunting, but it seems he is so good at it he is avoiding the game altogether. He has a good head and minds the responsibilities of town and home. He even aids in petty disputes well enough, and keeps a calm mind for talking. I would trust him with the people."

"Just not the enemy, eh? We are far in the woods for all things to be pleasant, captain."

"He holds a blade well," Bassar made the argument.

"Trained by the best I wager."

"He just seems timid around the matter."

"He'll be protecting us one day, I'm sure of it." They began a climb over a slope causing them both to pant by the effort. "Sooner would be better though."

They both laughed at themselves as they crested the slope and began to descend into a creek bed below the rise. Loose stones had been washed upon either bank so that the stream was flanked on either side by a wide shore. Bassar led them both downstream toward a long bend of the stream where there was a shallow that they could traverse and pass over the water safely to head back toward the village of Kurrum. "Looks quiet through the south hills. I didn't see anything," Bassar stated.

"Orc are probably worried about woods with most of them being watched by elves. Might not see any of their lot spill out of the Badlands, even if we are near the edge of the Empire."

"No vagabonds either. Borders seem safe today."

"That was already a long hike," Christof muttered. "We adding the lake yonder today?"

Bassar looked at the eastern tree line at the edge of the stony bank of the stream. He stroked his beard as he thought of climbing the distant hills upward, then scaling a cliff edge downward, then rounding the lake with its marshy shorelines, only then to return against those obstacles once again. He turned to look at his deputy and then he thought of how it might benefit them to make the trek this day. "We went north and got the Ash Mountain foothills-"

"West a ways and along the road to the edge of the woods," Christof added.

"We cut south through the hills and east to the creek. We will be checking the interior trail on the way back to Kurrum. Will you be ready to check the east lake at dawn?"

"Aye, captain. It'll give me a chance to get my mud boots too. Hate getting mirk water in my shoes this time of year."

"If we are just making the way east tomorrow we could get as far as the overlook too."

"Brambly back in there. Quite the excursion you've planned for us tomorrow."

"We can take Basimick with us, show him the route. I don't think he has seen the edge of the woods that way before."

"That would be good for him. Good for you too. Good for me also. Having him around takes your eye off me when I start to slow down a bit."

"Be ready for it."

"Ready at dawn, sir."

Bassar rested a hand on his companion's back, "Let us be off home then. Get some warm drinks before another cold morning comes calling."

They crossed the shallow creek, Christof using his spear to test the steps before he took them, when a noise tore through the tree line. Bassar drew out his blade and turned as quick as he was able but the beast was already upon him. A mountain bear, a large specimen among its kind, rose on its hind legs and swung a clawed paw at the captain. Chain from his mail was strewn about the rocks of the bank, leather from his jerkin ripped away in ribbons, and he fell with terrible force into the creek pebbles.

Christof heaved his spear but it caught along the muscular flank and left only a scratch before bouncing away. The mountain bear roared at the old soldier before taking Bassar into its maw, fangs biting deep into the upper leg and it wrenched him across the unforgiving stones. Christof took out his bow and pulled back as quickly as he could, releasing an arrow into the shoulder as he aimed for the creature's neck.

Blood spilled from everywhere and the stream became a red current. By prayer or through fear, the beast released, roaring as it backed away, and then with great speed it fled through the tree line back from where it revealed itself toward the eastern lake.

"Captain, oh captain," Christof kneeled with a heavy grunt. The wound was deep and torn, but with confidence the war veteran knew that with strength this would not be the end of Bassar. "Missed the important parts it did," he tried to reassure the wounded man. Christof dug into a pouch on his waist and withdrew a thin rope that he wrapped above the wound and tightened with a small rod. He lifted Bassar's coat of mail and was careful near the wound across his abdomen. "Good stuff, kept you safe. Just a bit of lost skin there, the worst bit is a lot of bruising maybe."

Bassar grabbed the shoulder of his companion, pulled on his cloak, but his grip weakened. "Hurts," was all he said between labored breathing and gritted teeth.

"Aye, and it will be a bit more too I think. Thank Christianna your lodge is close and ask Katrina to keep you light. I'm an old man after all."

"Lend me your walking spear."

"Aye, captain. Not much use it had as a weapon, did it? Didn't even stick on a good throw."

CHAPTER II
BLACKROOT WAKING

She was still asleep, ensnared in a dream-like world, but she knew that this vision was incredibly important. Vanessa herself was lovingly singing to her through the eaves of a summer canopy with a voice as sweet as a wild spring wind. It was a place that she had visited often over the many centuries and each time she was brought there she felt inspired. There was a low sun shining through the immense trees of the alien flora within the Goddess's realm of the Fey Wilde and it cast a comfortable warmth across a sky of dazzling colors. There were veins of spore capturing the light as though they were streams of clouds caught within a tremendous bright radiance, each tendril in the sky casting a new hue upon the forest world beneath them.

Suddenly there was a great division within the world and in front of her was a wide path that Vanessa could pass through. She was swept away, not knowing if she had been captured by servants of nature to be carried alongside Vanessa herself or if the magic of the Lady of Fey had altered the world so that her own stride could keep pace beside the Goddess. She knew the trees themselves could shift in this realm, perhaps it was the Fey Wilde itself that was moving around her, but the means of her travel mattered not, and she ignored whither she went and paid close attention only to the message of her Goddess, for Vanessa would not speak to her without purpose.

"I am called upon once more so soon," she asked.

Vanessa merely nodded as she had done in times of her calling before.

She noticed that the world of the Fey was quickly passing around her, as though her speed had become unmanageable. "Why do we travel at this speed? Is it that this task is important or that you need for this task to be done with great haste?"

The Fey Goddess nodded, affirming that both answers to her questions were true, and Vanessa led her deeper through the Fey Wilde into a territory that became more familiar.

"Why me and not another?"

The Goddess pointed to herself and this was enough to speak of the dangerous magnitude set before her.

Though no words were shared she understood what had been conveyed. "Destroy an immortal creature? But how can such a thing be done?"

Vanessa led her further still but the great Goddess was beginning to darken in mood and become pale in color as though she were shifting into the new season. The guest to the Fey Wilde was brought then to a great tree, one that she recognized, and within the bark was a powerful incantation, an illusion and charm that would disguise and misdirect those unaware of the spell. Beyond the clever enchantment, through the very trunk of the tree, was the head of a trail into a mountain pass that led to a grove protected by a narrowing in the rocky terrain. Hidden within the roots of the largest tree was revealed another incantation, more powerful than the last, which hid a cavern beneath the foundation.

"What is in here," she asked, unafraid to make such a request of the Goddess.

From Vanessa's hand were created many sprites that lit the air with a luminescent glow and they all flew into the cavern to lead the way. She was shown a dark room within the great mountain, tomes lined the walls and the shelves were to a height beyond the natural sight of the visitor. The sprites then directed her to climb against a column of the shelves and she pulled herself up the tremendous cavity that bore through the mountain toward the peak high above. Upon a shelf near the summit was a large book with a wide spine bound in fine leather that had still been aged despite incredible magic charms to preserve it.

"What will I need to find," she asked.

The book opened and within were ancient maps with names and markings so distant in their use that even she could not decode them from her centuries of life in the world. Inside were notes, handwritten pages with depictions of ancient things, but the details of everything were unclear and would require the book itself instead of the visions offered from the Fey.

"Who must I find," she asked, as all of this message was for one purpose only. As she turned to look away from the book the Fey Wilde took hold and moved her once again so that she was delivered back to the grove to stand before Vanessa. "Who is to be pruned for the greater good of the world," but as the answer was coming Vanessa began to brown, her form began to wilt, and then the veins within the Goddess became black as though she were a scorched plant. The dream world collapsed around the visitor and the Fey Wilde faded away.

Lilium awoke, disappointed that she was suddenly rebuked from within the Fey Wilde and that her question to the Goddess went unanswered. *That is not typical,* her mind calculated quickly. *Never has she abandoned me.*

Her eyes opened slowly and stayed narrow, her gaze sharp on the surroundings. There were others, she could hear them, the assassins who should be in a quiet slumber to listen for the Goddess's command, but they were distraught and restless. She could see one across from her, they were still strapped to their tree and they were writhing in broken nightmarish agony.

Quietly, as all the centuries of training allowed, she slipped out from her black-briar tree. The trunk was sloped to recline the elf in a cradle between its roots, and the branches hung over her in a thick basket of woven thorns. Carnivorous tendrils from cracks in the bark withdrew from her arms, legs, from about her neck, and some unlatched from across her cheeks as she left her bed. Barefoot, unencumbered, unhindered, she moved silently. Around her were the other Blackroot, trained assassins, special elves chosen by the Fey Goddess herself for divine tasks, but even as they were of the same order, she knew that the others were not like her.

At the base of the tree were her daggers, Blackroot blades that had been gifted to her from the Fey Wildes. They were decorated with embellishments of vines and thorns, inscribed with symbols from the Fey, and were razor sharp with a fine edge. Both daggers went into their rings kept on her belt before she moved on from her black-briar tree.

Lilium crept among the struggling assassins caught in their uneasy rest, wondering what had happened, but dreading what the answer may have been. "Terror," she whispered as she neared another of the Blackroot. She crawled up onto the reclining black-briar tree and used an open hand to touch the other elf's shoulder, moving a carnivorous vine away as she did. "Terror, awaken."

The other elf was shaken, caught in the dream of horror just as the others, and as she awoke the dark thoughts followed into her waking life. She prepared to cry out but Lilium viciously sealed the other assassin from making noise and took hold of her to disable any retaliation that the assassin's instinct would drive.

"Gentle, killer."

"Don't call me that, Lilium."

"Are you okay, Terror?"

"Not that either. I don't glorify this praise."

"Terica," Lilium corrected, smiling at the Blackroot as she fully woke. "What did you see? Did Vanessa say anything to you last night?"

"I'm not sure," Terica whimpered as the dream was brought to recollection. "I was near a woodland and then I remember seeing a victim that I had encountered before."

"Who," Lilium demanded.

"An old one. Someone that is already pruned." Terica took notice of the other Blackroot within the sacred grove and plucked several of the black-briar vines away from her flesh. They ripped away painfully and she wished her awakening had been more gentle. "Why do you ask such things? What did you see?"

"I was shown a library. It is hidden, but I know the way."

"There is a lot to find in a library-"

"And I know what to look for," Lilium pulled Terica to her feet. At the base of the tree Terica picked up her two Blackroot blades and they both made their way to the edge of the grove.

Terica whispered, "Is there a target?"

Lilium halted and she shook her head. "The vision ended before I was able to discover the target."

"What of the others?"

"Most of them don't speak anymore and I wouldn't trust them if they would wake from their nightmares. We must be gone."

"Have you seen this before, Lilium," Terica asked as she studied the others.

"Never." Lilium gave one last look at the other assassins in the grove. "Keep your daggers ready in case and let's try to be off before they wake."

"Two Blackroot?"

"Two of the best," but the compliment was ill received. "Come along, Terica. Two friends at least." Lilium gave a quick smile as the reluctant assassin became enticed to follow.

Quietly they slipped away from the hidden grove through passages in the wall of briar surrounding the resting place. As they entered the woods beyond the Blackroot grove, Terica glanced behind them and there appeared to be nothing more than a risky briar patch to hide where their den had been. Lilium tugged on her arm to get her attention and they both slipped away into the deep woods of Krethnarok.

CHAPTER III
HISSILANDA AND THE COUNCIL

She became silent but her radiant white glow did not cease and some shied away from her emanating light. Hissilanda stood before the other lords of the elven houses upon a stage beneath their thrones. They had all arrived to the woodland realm of Krethnarok, a forest that had stood as the honored center for all elvendom on Nhearn to discuss rumors of armies gathering under her orders. From the territories near the mountain ranges of Dol and Gor was King Dulfulad, a wood elf who had lived for nearly a millennium. His woodlands were far to the north of the dwarven kingdoms, beyond the sea, and his domain had remained isolated because of it. In the seat beside him was Queen Bilennia of the eastern borders, a collection of woodlands set around the Twin Rivers, whose trees gathered in dense groves across the distant edge of the East Border Spine. Bilennia was displeased to be called away from her homeland, for the orc hordes of the Badlands were kept at bay by her people's watch and too many had followed her away. Next to the queen was Seedgard, Lord of the South, whose kingly title had been lost when the Empire of Man had conquered the lands surrounding his own woodland home in the Imperial lands of Southrunn.

Dulfulad leaned back into the polished wood throne and looked down to the stage where stood Hissilanda who had finished her speech to all of them. "You dare to question the loyalty of the other elvenwoods, Queen Hissilanda, but it seems to us that your gathering of warriors is not in line with the missions of your other leaders. The orc in the east have already stretched thin the aid you would call upon from Queen Bilennia. My woods in the north are already at odds with territories there and the colonials from the Empire of Man. Southrunn is besieged on all sides by threat and our elvenwood is drafted into the efforts of the humans for their own plights. You would call on us to break a thin truce with the dwarves! You cannot use the Lady of the Fey as a call to gather our forces as your own armies."

"I am not gathering a force as a renegade element," Hissilanda sneered at Dulfulad. "Though, it would seem that the council has already passed judgment on my call to arms."

The queen of the borderlands leaned forward from her seat, "Queen Hissilanda the White, you do not have dominion over all elf kind because of your high seat. Krethnarok is still considered our most holy ground, but you cannot use such a position of leadership to pull together the resources of all your people and all your allies. We will not move forward to engage in such a costly attack on the dwarven nations." Bilennia leaned back in the seat and faced Dulfulad before airing, "Especially on faith alone."

Hissilanda glared at each member of the council before turning to the others present within the forum chamber. She smiled upon them and a radiant white glow of magical potency was cast from within herself upon them. She could see that there were supporters of her cause within the audience. There were many other elves of importance across the stage from the thrones, some who were militant elves, high seat delegates, and those of the lesser noble stratum. "What is it that the elves want," Hissilanda raised her hands to invite the others to speak. "Truly the views of their kings and queens are not the same as their people."

Dulfulad knocked the crook of his staff to the ground and demanded silence after an uproar came from the others seated within the large chamber. "Any more attempts to defy this council, Hissilanda, and we will not be required to linger here and listen to your pleas any longer."

Queen Hissilanda the White stood in the middle of the room and stared back at the king from the far north, "I would not wish to see your people taken from you." She had an arrogant confidence, "Join and lead us through to our rightful revenge or prepare to step aside."

"Hissilanda, control yourself," Dulfulad knocked his staff again.

"I demand by right, as Queen of Krethnarok, the High Seat of Vanessa herself, that all forces in elvendom be brought to my command. I intend to bring war over all the dwarves of Nhearn for the crimes they have committed against us!"

"Crimes we have no evidence of, Queen Hissilanda. We have no way to ground your accusations to any truth, and your claims are far too grandiose to be taken on any amount of faith. There is no possible way to hold your words accountable."

"Do you not feel this emptiness in your heart?"

"Feeling, Hissilanda, is not a truth," Bilennia added to Dulfulad's argument.

"It no longer matters," Hissilanda's mouth tightened with disdain. "I am the queen of Krethnarok and I call upon all elvendom to join my cause. They will join my banner if yours will not rise. They will seek our grand retribution." Others began an uproar that could not be quelled by the rapping of the king's staff.

"No, and that you continue to defy the council in this way-"

Hissilanda was quick to raise her voice against the outspoken king of the north, "The council has no authority to deny me or any elf this calling."

Dulfulad stood from the throne and waved his hand to quiet the queen, "You are not acting right, Queen Hissilanda. If you continue-"

"Then what will you do?"

Queen Bilennia of the borderlands then stood from her seat, "If her call to arms shall come anyway despite these talks then it should be resolved by this council now! I request that we remove Hissilanda the White from power; her title and her throne are forfeit. She will be removed and sent into exile."

Hissilanda did not show anything with exception to her continued contempt for the council, "If I am made to leave be prepared for a war unlike any that has ever been witnessed on Nhearn before now."

"Be silent, you have no power here any longer," Dulfulad said sternly from his seat. "You will from henceforth be known as Hissilanda the White alone, and no longer the Queen of Krethnarok. In the intermittent time this council will act according to custom and discover the next in favor of Vanessa."

"Have you heard nothing?" Hissilanda pointed at each member of the council, lingering most upon Dulfulad and Bilennia, "I hope you see that what is to come next you have all done to yourselves. Now my efforts will be doubled and my outcome will only be delayed by the moments wasted in words with you. War will come swiftly."

As Hissilanda stepped away from the stage and moved out of the council chamber several of the generals stood and followed behind her. Dulfulad looked about the room and believed that most of the others were unsure of how to proceed. "To any who follow her into exile from the borders of this woodland, know now that you will never be welcomed back to any land that we elves yet keep."

With the rapping of Dulfulad's staff, most of the room stood up and moved outside to join Hissilanda in the courtyard. Those who questioned where their loyalties lied were urged on by the elves who believed in Hissilanda to join with their queen. They were all now surely in exile, but they were all together and ready to follow their queen's call.

She left the doorway of the meeting chamber and went out to the shade of the great council tree where the elves of far places began to gather with her. Around Hissilanda were the lords and leaders from the four corners of the land whose people would rise to join the fight. She looked into the eyes of the members of the congregation and knew that they were likely to be the largest force assembled in all of Nhearn.

"We know that they mean well," said a princely elf whose presence hushed the murmuring crowd. "But what peace they wish to keep has already been lost. What lives they hope to save are already forfeit. Queen Hissilanda the White, the elves of the north have heard your call. We shall come."

"Prince Sylvarath, your father Dulfulad has exiled me. You would defy your kin to serve me?"

"The king of those woodlands should pay proper respect to our heart in Krethnarok, but he should also pay respect to his people. With his consent or without his blessing, our woodland banners will rise and answer to their queen."

Hissilanda touched his shoulder and he bowed, the elves of his lands doing the same behind him. "Upon my call," she said, "You and all of our kin shall empty to come south. Let no warrior be forgotten and let none able be left behind."

The elf from the third high seat, dressed in a suit of Imperial armor, a Southrunn elf whose lands were allied and taken to benefit the Empire of Man, bowed his head low. "We honor your call, Queen Hissilanda the White. Our woods may be disgraced in the eyes of our holiest forest, but our loyalty is and always has been to elvendom."

"Do not lay your head so low, Seedgard of the Empire, for mankind is a friend yet to our people. Together the Badland borders east of your region have been subdued and our own homeland kept safe. Even in your alliance you have kept strangers out of our sacred glades and the elvendom in the south is strong."

Seedgard took a knee followed by elves in Imperial dress behind him, "Please call upon us."

"I would be gladdened to have the elven realms of Southrunn answer to a higher purpose."

An elf dressed in dark clothing, whose appearance was much different than that of the other elven lands that chose to spread the jubilance of their homes with color in their vestment, stepped before the White Queen. Behind them were other elves whose faces had been tattooed with signs of spell craft and symbols of darkness. "What of the Sentinel Woodland? Would you accept the assistance of elves banished away until your calling?"

"No longer are the concerns among we elves alone," Hissilanda bowed her head slightly to the dark guests. "Agnithia will be welcomed to our cause and released from her punishments should she join with us."

"The Sentinel Queen has discovered many secrets for you in her time apart, my fair queen, and has taken the title and power of Witch-Heart from our Lady. She bids thee, take this gift with apologies that she sent us in her stead." A gnarled wooden orb, polished and smoothed by powerful magics, was presented to the queen as the elves of the Sentinel woods kneeled to her.

Hissilanda touched the shoulder of the dark leader among them, welcoming the Sentinel Woods under her banners. "Send word to Agnithia Witch-Heart that she will be a very important instrument in what is to come."

"With this, our queen, you may tell her yourself."

CHAPTER IV
THE LIBRARY

Terica was surprised that her companion had led them
only as far as the northern edge of Krethnarok where the
great peak of Aboraeve loomed over the forest. The
journey was short from the Blackroot groves in the heart
of the elven homeland and they moved quickly through
the woods, avoiding the clan sites and dwelling trees as
they neared the slopes of the great mountain. As they
passed north of the populated sites the two were able to
follow a common path through the forest that led to a
narrowing between two arms of the mountain. The trail
continued to climb uphill where it entered into the ravine
at the foot of the mountain. Guarding the narrow
passage was a lone tower to keep watch over the sacred
routes toward the peak and within was a single guard
who was adorned in silver armor. A white flag was
draped over the ledge which dazzled in the sunlight with
glimmering silver tassels.

"The White Queen's personal guard watches the
way to the Aboraeve," Lilium whispered to Terica as
they navigated the shrubs in the trees. "I only see one

guard though. For what purpose would the others be called away?"

Terica signaled that she was unsure.

"I still only see one," Lilium reached down to grab her blade from her hip.

"No," Terica grabbed Lilium's arm. "Is that the target?"

"They are in our way."

"They do not need to know that they are." Terica let go and retreated a step, unsure what the Blackroot assassin would do to her should they argue further.

Lilium surprised the other assassin as her hand fell away from the weapon, "What is your suggestion?"

"Are you not skilled at being unseen?"

"How dare you insult me," but the Blackroot's anger subsided when Terica smiled in jest. "I will have to get used to having a companion it seems."

"The tower only overlooks the ravine entrance," Terica stood up from behind the trunk of a large tree and attempted to look for other routes along the slope of the mountain. "It has a blind spot at the next crevice. We could climb to the route above."

They both crept along the tree line, weaving around bushes and shrubs to avoid rustling the vegetation. Lilium nudged Terica before they began up the slope, "That guard should thank you before we leave."

The two Blackroot were able to use the trunks of trees to climb the sharp slope and when the forest began to dwindle they made quick work of climbing the rocky cliff side. Beyond the sight of the tower they arrived at the path which carved up the side of the mountain back and forth to the upper elevations. Lilium would stop at times to make sure that their trail was still undiscovered but no one revealed themselves as they made their way upwards. As they at last crested the ridge over the foothills Lilium pointed into the vale below, "There!" She closed her eyes and prayed for answers from Vanessa but all she could use were the memories of her vision.

"Are you sure that is the right tree?"

Where Lilium pointed was a tree growing against the cliff and a narrow stone ledge allowed a treacherous passage toward it. "I am sure."

They continued to journey throughout the afternoon, traversing the loose rocks of the mountain slope to get to the narrow ledge, and as they arrived near the tree Terica could feel the powerful presence of the illusion. The roots of the tree were gripped into the rock, the thick trunk leaned against the cliff face, and the boughs were full of green leaves which shaded the area from the sun's light. "In the vision I saw that large trunked tree. There is a spell upon it, an illusion that hides a pathway behind it, and when we get through the passage it will lead to a grove and another such tree is hiding a cave behind yet another illusion."

They began feeling their way around the roots, knocking on the stone, and touching the bark to find where the illusion was hiding the passage through. Lilium found the hole, her hand falling through the illusion into the trunk causing her to stumble through the false image of the hidden tunnel. Once inside they quickly trekked through the grove, discovered the next tree, and passed through the illusion into the cave.

Though the darkness was near absolute within the cave they entered without hesitation, both assassins sharing the Fey touched eyes of the predatory Blackroot. The air became colder as they ventured deeper into the mountain and as they rounded a sharp turn within the cave they were surrounded by shelves of books. As Terica looked up she could see that the cave turned sharply upward and through the heart of the mountain was a deep cavity that must have neared the peak above. Encircling the cave all the way to the ceiling were shelves covered in books so that no more space could be made for new additions to the collection. "What is this place?"

"I believe it to be a very old library," Lilium answered as she tried to find a way to the upper levels of the cave. She gently attempted to climb the shelves, using her foot to gain height as if using a ladder, but the old wood gave way and sent an avalanche of books to the floor. "Very old."

"The book, you know which one it is?" Terica picked up several volumes that had spilled and she glanced over the texts.

"It is above," she pointed toward the top of the cavity. "I will know it when I see it, but it will take me some time to retrieve it." She tried getting a foothold on another shelf, hoping that the fixtures might hold. After several attempts she managed to find some shelves that could hold her and she began to climb.

Terica waited below, not sure that she would be much help in the heights of the library, and she opened more books as Lilium's effort threw more of the ancient tomes from above. "These are not about Krethnarok, Lilium," her voice echoed up into the chamber. There wasn't an answer as Lilium struggled to find a safe passage, but Terica continued to explain to her companion, "There are songs of the High Elves in these books. They must have perished thousands of years ago?"

Terica gently picked up another book which had fallen so that the pages had smashed into the ground. After a moment she called up to Lilium, "This one is about the far north during the Great War! These could have been written over three thousand years ago!"

Her excitement began to overwhelm her and she tried to look at every book that had fallen, attempting to date the names of heroes, calamities, events, and phenomena from what history she knew from her other studies. As hours passed Terica had read many passages from the tomes and she stacked the books against the shelves respectfully as she completed skimming over them. As one book fell from the higher shelves she dove to catch it, hoping that it could have been older than even the books close to the floor. "This one is about Krethnarok," she said disappointed, but as she opened the book it unfolded with the tale of the Sentinel Woods and the breaking of the alliance. "This happened only a few decades ago."

Terica closed the book and looked up to avoid being hit by yet more tomes and as the higher shelves rained down they revealed events across Nhearn that had occurred within the last few years. "Have you found it," she shouted with a new worry that someone might be inside the library with them.

After a few more moments there was an echoing shout from above, "I've found it!"

Terica sat and waited for her companion to return, taking the time to read additional stories, trying especially to discover tomes that dated far back into antiquity. When at last Lilium returned to the bottom of the cavity she revealed the book. It was larger than any of the other books, it was bound in a cover of thick treated leathers, and it exuded a static power that they both knew to be powerful magic. There was no title or note upon the cover to give a purpose and there wasn't a way to guess the age of the tome for the magic had preserved it well.

"You are well read," Lilium asked, taking notice of the many books that had been stacked around her companion.

"I am," Terica replied proudly. "Do you know what information you are looking for?"

"A location. I believe there should be a map somewhere and maybe we can discover what secret resides there."

Terica opened the book and she glanced at Lilium with worry.

"What is it?"

"The other books are a mix of sylvari elven and Imperial common."

"What is this one?"

"This symbol," she pointed at the middle of the page, "It's a dwarvish script."

"You know dwarvish?"

"Some, but this one," and her finger moved to the next symbol, "It's Nüddish. This next one is sylvari elven, and then there are plain skrits in here, and Imperial common, and this one isn't even used in writing at all. It's all in cypher."

"It doesn't say who wrote it?"

"All of these are in the same hand," Terica waved around the room. "There is only one author and they never wrote their name."

Lilium picked up one of the loose books and compared it to another before taking a long look at the entire library. "It would take an Age for one person to make all this."

"Longer," Terica nodded to the book that Lilium was holding. "That is about the beginnings of the Empire of Man."

"That would be more than six millennia ago. This place must have had multiple hosts." As she opened the book she quickly closed it back up with worry, "The same damn hand wrote this as well."

"Vanessa perhaps," Terica considered. "It was she who led you here."

"Wild thoughts of the Fey would explain the cypher." Lilium returned to her companion who was still moving through the pages of the mystical book. "There," her hand captured the page before it could be turned. Upon it was a map but it was detailed in the mysterious codes. "Can you tell me where this is?"

"It uses a very archaic style of mapping, and the names are all written in changing letters, but I believe it says Dark Spire."

"What is there?"

Terica turned the book to see if there were notes, flipped the page to see if she could decipher any of the passages with useful information. "High Elves?"

"Do you know anything about them?"

"Little except what is passed around in legend, but there is a book there that has some information about them," Terica pointed to a small book set on top of a stack that she had set aside for her amusement. "And only one passage of Dark Elves."

"Dark Elves? I've never heard of such a thing."

Terica returned to the passage in the large book, "It says we need to be there at the rise of the sun." She took a moment to change between the many symbols, some phonetic, some iconographic, and with excitement she shouted, "At sunrise, there is a secret path on the south wall."

"Where does this path lead?"

"The, uh," she rubbed her eyes to think. "The Bastion? It is a marker, or a tower, maybe just a landmark of some kind, and then the map continues passed that, but that is the last detail."

"Nothing about what is there for us?"

"Only what we need to see to get there it seems. This passage, a poem I think, I am not sure if it says a shadow, or a remnant of evil, or a sinner, or," her voice trailed again as the book refused to reveal its secrets. "Is this the target?"

"No," Lilium said with surety. "This place will only reveal what I need to prune the target."

"I believe this area on the map is the Green Bay. That is far in the east, in the Forbidden Lands."

Lilium nodded and Terica closed the book, "Then that is where we are heading. Let us be away from this place."

CHAPTER V
DEPARTURE OF SYLVARATH

The elven prince from the northern regions gathered his guard and prepared for the departure from Krethnarok when an agent of the queen arrived at the upper boughs of the dwelling tree. They wore silver armor entirely and had a white cape to match the mystical glow of their leader, the ensemble entirely symbolic of the White Queen's influence, though the uniform was vastly unique from any other elven decorum. The agent did not speak but gestured for the guards of the prince to step aside. The silver clad soldier handed the letter only to the prince who took it without a word and the agent departed without ceremony. The parchment was rolled, clasped with a silver ringlet, and sealed with sacred tree wax from the trees of deep Krethnarok. He opened the queen's correspondence immediately:

> *With great haste head to your homeland. Seek the routes of the Plain Elves to move you with speed that you might return your route south quickly. Bring with you the Dark Matter from your holds. It has been vaulted by your father for the dangers it carries to elfkind, but its potency will be useful among the dwarven holds. Do not touch them for the risk of your own survival.*

*Attack first then from the sea. Strike at Malenclutch
and seek passage into the Cradle. Do so swiftly, for all
the generals must strike with such speed that Arrumklad
is unaware until the end.*
Leave none behind you, General Sylvarath.

"So it is then," Sylvarath rolled the letter and placed
the ringlet back around it.

One of his guards approached as the letter was
rolled away. "What does the queen command?"

"She commands me to command. I am to be
designated as one of her generals in the effort against the
dwarves."

The guards adjusted to stand proper and they bowed
to respect the newly awarded authority. "Who are the
others to take command?"

"I am unsure." Sylvarath looked around the
dwelling tree and then stepped out to the outer branches
where he could look down into the glades of the elven
city. There were gatherings of the other nobles speaking
of what was to come and throngs of visiting elven clans
were already moving into the paths out of Krethnarok.
"Whoever her other leaders might be, they have offered
her much."

"What do you mean, my lord?"

"The White Queen seems to know a great many
things, even very old secrets. The caves in the dead
mountains are still sealed, are they not?"

"The old tombs? Beyond the forest boundary? The
king Dulfulad has forbidden even venturing there and
his predecessor had closed them an Age ago."

"She knows what is in there." He took a moment to
consider who else might know of the ancient place in his
homeland or the contents within that were still a mystery

38

to even himself. "Let us be off with haste. We travel light and at speed for as long as we can. There is no time to waste as we make the venture back north."

"Lord, the king could not-"

"We leave without him. He stays in Krethnarok."

CHAPTER VI
THE WATCHER'S REUNION

Lissuana entered the tower through the front door, having it open and close with only a playful nod. She walked in with tattered sandals that slapped on the tile and her staff, which had been worn on the bottom with spans of traveling, echoed with each knock upon the ground. Around her were trophies, keepsakes, displays of curiosities, and oddities from ages past. The interior was like a museum, a treasury, and a vault, but all these things she walked passed without a glance. Her large book which had a sling stitched to its spine flung about as she wandered with a happy skip in her step, adding an oddly gleeful presence in the otherwise dreary castle.

The lord of the castle and keeper of the tower came with a somber air from the far side of the hall. "Your energy is ruining my gloomy tower, Lisa."

"Just a small offering before I head on my way again, Calcifor. You should be happy that I am the one visiting though, your sister would have brought a much worse atmosphere than I."

"Addonna? Dread is a tad different from gloom. I suppose I should consider myself lucky." As they met at last in the long corridor they embraced as old friends. "Why have you come, Lisa? Why did my guard not send you away?"

"They were all very capable, but skill can only go so far when dealing with me," Lissuana let out a chuckle.

"They were all meant to hunt for witches anyway." Calcifor led her into the deeper chambers of his castle until they arrived at the scenic room where he had made his study. The dim chambers of the castle seemed far darker after he opened the doors into the bright space which was illuminated with large open windows facing a lovely view of the rugged coast and ocean. "You still haven't told me why you are visiting, Lisa."

"I just wanted to check on you."

"You have been meddling again," Calcifor wagged a finger to jest. "Prendrick will have more to say about your affairs than I."

"I am not to meddle, but you can operate an Auroran cult?"

"Cult? You say it with such a hiss." Calcifor leaned into a chair beside a window. "I am merely adjacent, and at times they ask for my sage advice." He drew the tips of his fingers together as his gaze wandered to the ocean.

"Well, may I do the same?"

"So that is why you have come then." He nodded, though he became visibly concerned over what query she could be bringing with her.

She hesitated and the glee faded from her to match the tower's gloomy demeanor. "I believe that I have found it again."

A long moment passed until Calcifor realized what she meant and after the look of surprise he became serious, "It is useless."

Lissuana shook her head and wagged a finger back at him, "I found it and the wielder."

41

"Have you now." Calcifor glanced at an object which he kept at the center of the room. "I may have found a wielder as well, though I know not when they will make their appearance or when they might find themselves in possession of it. All I am aware of is that they will come here to this very castle."

"Am I wrong to make sure that this one lives?"

"Well, that depends," Calcifor leaned forward. "Do we Watchers document for the next coming, or do we protect Nhearn for the next coming? Do the old oaths still mean anything? What is our purpose after all these years?"

"Muddled it seems, especially for the few we have left on our side. And what if there isn't another coming? I wasn't expecting to be a Watcher for so long." She sighed deeply and started to take notice of Calcifor's gaze around the study. "What do you think?"

"I can tell you what my sister would say."

"I haven't come to be scolded," Lissuana's eyes followed his gaze and fell upon the center of the study where a pedestal stood lonesome. Over the top of it was draped a thin black sheet over what appeared to be an orb beneath it. "Have you been moving pieces?"

"I have, and I am."

"Meddler," she accused jokingly. "What are you doing?"

"Preparing, I hope."

"Has this future orb told you anything?" She moved closer to it before he stood up from his chair and waved her away from it. "Have you seen anything at all?"

"Nothing helpful," he shuttered. "Only dread."

"Don't pay it much mind," she said as she corrected her posture away from the pedestal. "The future has brightness in it somewhere." They both stared at the hidden orb, worried that what it had offered could have been the truth. "Sometimes it's as simple as perspective, maybe, and I imagine that the paths we choose change what that thing would say to us. Nothing is lost yet."

"Was I wrong to question it?"

Lissuana shook her head gently. "I would have looked at the orb too; maybe I would have even seen it in the same way as you." She smiled at Calcifor, "But the future has never been a commandment. We have seen far too much of it to know that."

"Don't tell the others that I broke the oaths."

"Wouldn't want them to think that I had either."

He sat back down in the chair beside the window, "Don't tell them that I used it either, or that I was caught despairing."

"I wouldn't even know who to tell."

He took a deep breath and tried to smile, "The world is in good hands while you can carry the hope for all of us, Lisa."

CHAPTER VII
BASIMICK OF KURRUM

Away from the troubles of the Empire, in the heart of the Ash Wood, Basimick contended with the chill autumn air as he completed his morning routine. He placed a log upright once again and struck it with the axe that was now beginning to dull with use due to the season's wood harvest. The log splintered to either side and he grabbed yet another log to split on the chopping stump. The rhythm continued, heavy heaves overhead with an old axe driving into the stump followed by the sound of kindling piling together after each successful swing.

At last he felt that enough firewood was made to keep the hearth lit inside for the day and enough of it was left over to contribute to the winter stores. He drove the axe one last time into the stump and hope of a free afternoon was all that he had on his mind. He gathered one of the piles of wood and stacked it hastily into the stockpile under an awning safe for winter. With the other pile he began to haul as much as he could manage in each trip to the door of the lodge, tucking splinters under each arm, and he stacked it in a rush by the front door. A final armful and he braved to go inside the lodge where his sister was sure to have more tasks that he could do.

The cool air snuck in with him and he could see the draft from the open door strike his father with a violent shiver. Basimick moved beside the hearth and carefully began to unload his arms as quietly as he could, both not to wake his father and also to avoid his sister. The effort was futile.

Tera came into the room and set a broth soup into her father's lap, "Keep your strength up and have this. It will help keep the cold away." She turned to her brother, "Are you done with the chores?"

"Just these last few bits of wood here," he continued quietly and slowly to avoid her suspicion.

"There isn't much else then, but if you could help with a run into town, I'd appreciate it."

With luck a free evening could still be had. "What is it?"

"Check if any of the merchants have some medicine. Father is doing well but I don't want a cold or infection setting in when the first real chill comes this year."

Bassar stirred out from under the blankets and drew the broth to his mouth. "Cold isn't what will stop me," he claimed.

Basimick looked up and managed to save a bit of wood from leaving his grasp before hitting the floor. "Mind if I take some time after?"

"Be back before dark is all. Do stay out of trouble," she added with a knowing glare.

Basimick finished stacking the wood with sudden fervor and he collected several deer pelts from the drying racks.

His father squinted at the pelts, "Soon you'll have to hunt some of your own. You're good at the rest of it, best tracker we have in Kurrum, you just need to have the heart to take the shots."

"How are you today, father," he asked while preparing himself for the trip to town.

"Fine. Your sister worries too much."

Basimick tied his nicer boots up and dusted off a tunic he reserved from work or chores. "Someone should worry for you if you won't do it yourself. Not too many people would get attacked by a bear and then pray for work."

"Prayer, bah."

"Pray you should. Gods must be watching you for only a wounded leg. Anyone less than you would have certainly perished."

Bassar waved his son away, "Leave your prayer for my funeral and request the Gods to answer how to hold me in the grave."

Both of them laughed until Tera came back with a scolding look at both of them. "Go off then if you're ready, Basimick. Light fades fast this time of year."

He was not often offered an open afternoon, and less often an errand so simple. Basimick heaved the pelts over his shoulder and with his free hand he took up his simple guardsman sword before heading out the door. He crossed through the lodge clearing, went over a small wooden bridge above the creek that hugged around the lodge, and entered into the Ash Wood. At this time of year the leaves were vibrant reds or bright golden hues so that every hour of the day glinted with wondrous and natural perfection. The ground off the trail was not packed or mismanaged by shrubs, but was an open scape littered with mossy rocks that had been made pleasantly flat with years of autumn sheds.

As he ventured down the trail from home he came at last to the road which led west out of the Ash Wood borders and east to the gate of Kurrum. The road was not much wider than to allow a single cart to pass, but there were few visitors to the small quiet village. The narrow road weaved through the gentle hills and through the local ash trees until it met an old wooden gate affixed to a simple palisade that kept the village defended from roaming deer or pesky squirrels, though it could certainly not withstand much more. The wall was made in a wide ring around Kurrum from a tall western butte, starting from the rocky south rise, and it ended at the sheer north face of the village's bluff. Inside the ring was a gathering of homes made from the local lumber. Few homes were larger than a single room, but each one hosted a fenced garden plot and wood pile for winter, though each was smaller in stock than his own, which he took note of.

With the guardsman sword sheathed at his waist it was hard not to notice Bassar's son as he passed through the little village. Basimick waved at the people who saw him, which were many, for every home in Kurrum was built so that the front door faced one of the two roads that ran throughout the village. There was the Mainroad, a wide dirt pathway that went to each end of Kurrum, west at the main gate which he had entered from and east to a large dwarven doorway at the foot of the butte which he could see clearly from the other side of the village. At the midpoint of Mainroad was Crossroad, so named that it crossed the Mainroad, and it ran the length of the village from north to south.

Basimick continued along his way to the village center and it was where both roads met that the denizens of Kurrum gathered at what they called the Midway. It was there at Midway that some locals with a passion for trade had set a ring of simple booths and stalls around the village well. There at the market, the local hunters and gardeners could sell with the occasional merchant who would pass through the village while traveling between more prominent places. On this day there were many about trying to stock up on supplies brought in for the winter months and the two roads were congested. He managed his way through them and as he drew near the ring of market stalls he could hear his name being called over the murmur of the town center. "Basimick! Basimick, over here!"

"Enough shouting, Marccus."

"Just worried someone would outbid me on those pelts."

"Nonsense, unless you've heard they're paying double?"

"Don't let them hear you. I am sure they would," Marccus laughed. He helped Basimick lay out the pelts over the stall counter and began to look at each one with a close eye. "I say this is fine work. Better than some of the other seasoned hunters, though they also sell more of the meat."

"They will regret it in the winter. I will be well fed."

"Cold though," Marccus jested.

"I've enough firewood for that. For now I just need enough sovereigns for a vial of medicine."

"Is your father not doing well?" Marccus didn't mean to cause a ruckus but the whole of the town center was a mess of shifting and shushing to hear what news they could have of their beloved Bassar.

"No-"

Gasps and wailing fell about the place.

"No, I mean that he is well." Basimick twisted about so that everyone could hear him, "He is well!" Everyone hushed, nodded, smiled at each other, and then continued on their way. He spoke softly to Marccus, "It's my sister, she just wants to be prepared is all."

"A wise idea. I believe Monice may have some on hand," he pointed across the way to a stall few others would dare to get caught visiting.

"The elf?"

"A wise lady, like your sister. She can usually heal what ails you, for a few sovereigns of course," Marccus counted out some coins and handed them over to Basimick. "Two each?"

Basimick nodded and took the coins eagerly, "If I hear four each tomorrow-"

"Then I owe you some sovereigns."

Basimick was becoming impatient and could only think about running off as his tasks drew near to an end, but beyond neurotically touching the pommel of his sword at each step he managed his outward excitement. As he crossed the Midway he shook hands and smiled, saying quick hellos to avoid long conversations. He walked up to the quiet stall that was set on the southwest corner, as far away from the dwarven gate as possible. "Hello," Basimick nervously said with a genuine smile.

"What's this then," the elf brought a judging finger to her cheek. She was dressed in a fine blue robe that had at one time been regal but had now faded with time and had been bleached by long hours of standing in the sun. "Are you here for business, young guardsman?"

"I am. I happen to be looking for medicine. My father is hurt, not near death you understand, but his leg is having issue."

"I may have something." She ducked under the stall only a moment and returned with two handfuls of small glass vials filled with all manner of colorful liquids, each capped with a cork and sealed in wax that was stamped with an official Imperial apothecary sigil. "Do you need more wards for infection, or for pain, or maybe a curative for the common cold?"

"I admit, I am unsure. I'd imagine a bear bite would need all three, but," He held out the ten coins and looked at the vials with shame.

"A bear bite?"

Basimick nodded.

"I apologize. I should have seen it. You are Bassar's son? The Captain is free to have these."

"You're jesting. I couldn't accept that."

Monice laughed, "I am sure you will earn your favors in time, but this is one I do for Bassar. There is a long lasting feud beyond the forest here and he has kept the peace between the dwarves and myself. The human Empire is interesting in that it allows so many among its numbers, but your father is the reason I own this simple stall in Kurrum. He also saved my life in Havvel. I owe him so much more than just a simple remedy."

"Havvel? My father doesn't speak of it."

"A most terrible calamity. I hope the memory fades soon. Thankfully he brought us all to Kurrum, even if there are dwarves. Conflict keeps peaceable elves like myself in hardship. You are my first customer, with the exception of the town bishop."

"Then please, take five sovereigns, I have no need and you can owe me one small favor so that when I'm bit by a bear your medicine can aid me too."

She took the coins, "And to whom do I owe this small favor?"

"Basimick of Kurrum," he said proudly, hand on the hilt of his sword.

"I am sure you will have much finer titles by the time you call upon my favor."

Basimick took each bottle, put them in his coin purse gently, and then he gave a bow and a smile that Monice honored in kind. As he left he could hear her trying to sell her wares to the crowd around her, shouting, "Good enough for Bassar, well enough for you!"

Tasks completed, he took haste eastward down the rest of Mainroad and found the usual band of dwarves gathered by the entryway. They were sitting about on stumps they had rolled up against the butte wall and had their pipes of vanilla scented tobacco billowing while several of them sang in old dwarvish or played on their flutes and liars.

Even in his youth Basimick was already head and shoulders taller than the dwarves, though his chin was bare and his arms, while strong, were notably scrawny compared to the burly limbs of the stone carvers. They looked up at him from under bushy eyebrows, their stern eyes and robust nose were the only noticeable bit of face. All else was covered by the mess of hair that had either been left in wild disarray or quelled with braids and oils as only a dwarven beard could manage.

Their instruments sounded tinny and boisterous, but it paired pleasantly with their deep raspy singing voices and they all seemed entranced by their own tune as Basimick approached. The oldest among them raised his hand to halt the band and he stroked his beard that had only recently begun to show gray. "Ho ther' young master. How is your da then? Not seen him since that fateful morn." Smoke was billowing from his lips as he spoke and it clung to his beard like a mountain mist.

"He does well. My sister keeps him indoors mostly."

"A wise lass. I be betting he'd keep going til his grave comes to call if that daughter a' his would not be demanding him take seat. I do hope him well wishes."

"Well wishes," the other dwarves chimed in to echo their elder.

The old dwarf took a few puffs from the long stem of his pipe and asked, "What can we humble folk do for the Captain's son here then?"

Basimick took the loop of the scabbard from his belt and handed the sheathed sword, hilt first, to the dwarf. "I have five sovereign here now. You had told me once it would be three for you to sharpen it up."

"Aye, and what for the other two coin ther' then? You know better than to tell a dwarf 'bout extra monies." He laughed and the smoke cloud nearly covered his whole self as it billowed forth from his chest.

"I have a wood splitter at home that's getting dull."

The dwarf stood up from his stump but was not much taller than when he had been sitting down. "Aye, lad. Bring yer axe and yer coin and I will oblige." The older dwarf then put his thick fingers in his mouth and gave a sharp whistle that forced the others up to their feet. "Anvil and whetstone aren't far, boy. Come on, but keep close, aye."

"I get to go in?"

"Guard of Kurrum is welcome. This ain't the Cradle after all, is it."

In single file they marched in through the square doorway. They traveled down the forward hall into a large chamber lit by basins of fire that were hung like fancy chandeliers near the ceiling that was carved quite tall for the stature of dwarves. Basimick looked about and saw the maze of tunnels, some leading to dark corners and others heading toward torch lit distances. At the middle of the central chamber was a round rise, much in the shape of a large wide well, but it was filled with hot glowing embers. Beside this was a wealth of smithing tools strewn about in a way that gave no pattern or yielded any respect for the practice. Nevertheless the dwarves went to their craft. One took the blade and set it to the ember while others set out to find hammers and grinding stones before taking their places around an old iron wrought anvil.

"Oh, just a bit of sharpening," Basimick said as the metal began to heat.

A dwarf spoke in their tongue and the elder gave a wink and a nod. "Swords bent and dinged. Can't go and be havin' guards in our town wanderin' with scrap."

As the hammers began to soothe the old battered blade back into its shape of prestige, Basimick started to look around at the smooth walls of the chamber. At the height of his chest was a line of dwarven runes that continued throughout the chamber and lined every hallway. "What is this here," he whispered to his old dwarven chaperone.

"Dwarvish runes to ward off wizards and witches. We stout folk aren't so keen on the use of magics. It was long ago when we made our marks so that ther' was no need to worry 'bout it. Any odd spell or what not gets stolen away from the air 'fore it comes."

"Vanishes?"

"Helena knows where, though she tells us not."

"The dwarven God?"

"A Goddess who lives in the stone. She is the earth, and we dwarves love all things earth. Gem and metal, but she loves the strong meats of granite most. She cares for us dwarves and we do our share to honor her."

"It is all very interesting."

"Kurrum doesn't seem to have much taste for religion. Us folk here don't do too much, but we offer small words at night. 'Nough to comfort ourselves," he laughed under his breath and the smoke covered the runes for a moment before stagnating into a vapor around the room. He pointed back to the runes so his thick finger poked the stone, "Helps a lot with the wild magics of elves. Keeps the dwarven forts clear of stray fire and bolt."

"A blessing," Basimick said and rubbed it, perhaps for luck, though he now wished the tension of elves and dwarves wasn't lingering on his mind.

"Aye, it is." The old dwarf sighed and Basimick could tell the same tension was also on his mind. Smoke was caught in his whiskers as he let out a very deep breath, as though the weight of that thought was being pressed onto his shoulders. "Sounds like the hammering is done. Must be ready then." He looked at the blade to inspect a proper dwarven quality. "Very good here, brothers." He passed the blade on to Basimick, hilt first, "And here you are, lad."

Basimick inspected the sword as best he could, though his eyes were not as trained as the dwarves, and he said, "Should serve me quite well. Many thanks to you all."

"Guards have much to do 'round here. I am sure rogue tree limbs and the imaginings of will-o-wisps won't know what hit 'em."

Basimick smiled, "Or a bear."

The dwarves all looked at each other and fell silent as Basimick left the room and darted out from the tunnels under their butte.

CHAPTER VIII
THE IMPERIAL HUNTERS

Basimick nodded to the citizens as he wandered down the Mainroad toward the western gate. They smiled at him, some thanked him for taking up the sword for Kurrum, and many asked him to wish his father good health. He grabbed the hilt of his blade to keep it from swinging on his hip and he would tell them that he would do his best for the village, knowing that the only danger now was out in the woods waiting to strike again. He bowed at the watchtower beside the gate and an old guardsman now manning the post returned the same to him.

As he left the gate he started to jog, excited to be off on his own adventure doing a patrol around the south creek bends. He turned to the trail back to his father's lodge and passed near the bridge back to his clearing. "They wish you well, father," he said aloud. "And I will make sure this never happens again." He continued following the creek as it flowed into the southern regions of Ash Wood, creating the imaginary path in his mind that his father and the other guardsman had taken from the stories they had been telling.

After some distances south he came to a space where the waters leveled into a calm shallow pond that was hugged on either side by a wide shore of river rock. Basimick looked around until he found the deep gouges in the banks of the stream. This was where the bear had struck. It was on the opposite bank when it had taken notice of his father and another village guard, then it charged across the shallows, took Bassar's leg in its maw, pulled him through the water and across the stones before letting him go at last. Basimick had heard the story several times now and he looked for the exact spot where it had happened.

A clear patch swept up in the blanket of leaves, blood yet washed away by the weather, the scraps of broken chain armor, and bloodied leather strips littered an area larger than Basimick expected. The combat must have been worse than his father's tall tales implied. He knew that the other guard that day had then shot the bear over the shoulder when it decided to let his father go and it retreated back toward the foothills.

He followed the trail of the bear's retreat to the water's edge and he slowly crossed the shallows to avoid wetting his boots. On the other side the marks continued, just as easy to follow, out into the trees. He was able to move quickly, years of tracking the local deer made following a panicked bear an easy venture. He raced eastward and rose up into the foothills. He paused for a moment in a clearing of ash trees and looked skyward to get the sun. *There is still time in the day yet.*

Basimick went deeper into the Ash Mountain foothills and stopped again when he arrived at a sharp rise that dropped away suddenly at its peak to a cliff that sank into the murky waters of a large lake. He bent down to see what path the bear had taken, hoping it might have avoided the fall into the swamp and turned north to the easier shore. Suddenly a whistle sounded, but it wasn't a bird, nor a signal from a guard of

Kurrum. It was sharp but above him was a thundering crack as the trunk of a tree erupted into splinters.

He fell backwards and grabbed the hilt of his sword hoping that his nerves would settle quickly and he could get his wits back about him. The tree nearby had been shot, perhaps by magic, and the leaves fell around him in a cloud. The trunk was split in two and branches had fallen from the strike. *What is out here,* his thoughts began to lean away from fear and bent toward curiosity. He got to his knees and neared the edge of the cliff where he could see over the lake beneath him.

Although the canopy of the ash trees covered most of the view below, a column of smoke rose above the trees somewhere on the southern shore. It was the frontier lands and the plume could mean anything. Basimick's mind raced from a dangerous forest fire, to the possibility of simple travelers, or even that it could be wild orc from the far eastern Badlands. He looked again at the sun and guessed on the time to get back home. He glanced at the bear trail that he could now see went off toward the north and he looked back at the plume of smoke to the south.

After a moment he chose an easy path down the face of the rocky cliff and made his way through the murky swamp shallows to the south shore. *Neither a bow nor a companion to fight a bear,* he thought to ease his mind from leaving the dangerous hunt. Vengeance or bravado, neither came to him now that curiosity had taken hold.

Basimick drew near the plume and then crept quietly toward the smoke, hand to the hilt of his blade in case any dreadful orc would spring forth. He arrived at the edge of a small clearing but he did not find any orc there, instead there were two men dressed in strange leather jerkins and fine chainmail armor. They had tall boots that were crusted with travel and weathered by trauma. Basimick inspected them and saw that they were well armed, each having a sword at the waist, a dagger beside it, another dagger in their boot, a small axe with a curved handle that did not appear useful for chopping wood, and strapped to their backs were heavy spiked cudgels. Inside their encampment were more weapons still: sets of swords in any length desired with any broadness needed, bows and arrows labeled neatly with force, distance, and a number seemingly unrelated to the added variety of munitions in every style of head, fletch, and shaft. There were also maces and flails in fluted, spiked, and barbed stylings. They had enough with them to arm a whole township, but there were only two bedrolls and a few sacks of food.

The most interesting weapon the men had brought however, and the item that possibly told the most of why they were here, was a machine that they both were desperately working with on the beach. They cranked and pulled but seemed angered or at times nervous about it. The contraption was not much taller than their waists and it leaned on two wheels at the forward of its boxy foundation. Long handles were anchored into the sand at the rear of the base and it seemed as mobile as a large wheelbarrow. On its top were two long arms pulled almost to breaking by a heavy metal wire made taut by a crank and gear. It was a giant crossbow, an Imperial scorpion weapon rarely seen beyond the sieges of the olden days.

The men put a metal javelin spear into the groove and with a tug of a lever the bow released the test shot over the lake. It was so fast it was nearly invisible, but a sharp whistle revealed whither it traveled until it made a sudden stop on the far side of the lake. After a moment the music twang of the bow string subsided and it was followed by the thundering sound of a cracking tree echoing over the waters. "Much straighter," one of them cheered.

Basimick was impressed by the weapon and as the two men stood about their campfire to congratulate themselves he left his hiding spot to reveal himself to them. "I am Basimick, son of Bassar, who acts as the captain of the watch in these woods. By Imperial Law, identify yourselves." It was his first time accosting woodland wanderers and he tried to be as professional as he possibly could.

"Hold there, we mean no grievance." The shorter of the two pushed the taller and both of them showed their empty hands to Basimick. "Let me get this settled right away here," the short one said and reached into his belt sack. "Here we are now," and he showed a large metal coin of his official Imperial status. "Also this writ from the Empire."

Basimick let go of the hilt of his sword and showed his empty hands to the others and everyone took a deep breath as the tension lifted from the camp. "What is this here," Basimick asked.

"Official business for the honor of the Emperor himself." The short fellow put the coin away and held out the document. Basimick took the letter and was as thankful as ever that his father had taught him to read. It was written:

> *Let it be known that the holder of this*
> *official seal be an instrument of the*
> *Empire with commandment as high as the*
> *Emperor's own demands. All costs of*

*lodging or provisions shall be
compensated by the Imperial Sovereign.
Consider all legal issues to be under the
direct action of the Emperor's decree. Do
not hinder or prevent actions from any
member of this company or befall action
for treason against the Empire. Official
title of status: Dragon Hunter.*

On the opposite side was listed a sizable reward for discovering and returning the official coins, and if at all possible the remains of the carrier of this writ to any hold within the Empire, in addition to an official wax seal stamped by the personal signet of the Emperor himself.

"Dragons?"

"A big one too," the tall one said. "We hope it stopped in these hills but we haven't been so far west since the chase out of the southern Badlands."

"Did you say captain's son?" The short one tucked the Writ safely back into his belt sack. "You hear of any odd things or perhaps even see a large flying terror nearby?"

"Can't say that I have."

"Heard any rumors of such an occurrence, perhaps?"

"No," but Basimick suddenly realized his original mission then. "My father was actually attacked recently by a mountain bear and-"

"Terribly sorry for your loss, sir," they both said in unison with their heads low.

"No, he is well. Leg could be better, but what I mean is this was a mountain bear. They stay in the east near the edge of the Ash Wood. It is a rare thing when they come down from the mountains. I haven't heard of it in my lifetime anyway."

The two looked at each other and then northward and eastward. The mountains and hills before them were gaining long shadows in the late evening sun. "Is there a settlement near here?"

"Just north. Go west to the creek and follow it upstream. It flows right through the middle of town."

"Is there lodging by chance?"

"We could accommodate for official dragon hunting business," Basimick said excitedly.

Basimick helped to dismantle the weapon and to his surprise the two were more than happy to talk at length about the machinery and its use. He heaved the heavy pieces into the cart and then offered to help pull the heavy thing over the cliff. After the difficult dredge through the muck and the hazardous climb over the lip of that rocky hill they came to the creek. They crossed over the shallows with little struggle and the rest of the way north to Kurrum was without hassle. They found the road as they neared the borders of Kurrum and they wove in and out of the ash trees. They dragged the cart around a wide bend until they arrived at the western gate of the small village where his sister Tera stood waiting in the waning twilight.

"The sun has set, Basimick," she said first before anyone else could speak.

"Beg your pardon, ma'am. He has helped us greatly. We imagined ourselves far from friendly places." The taller of the two took the handles from Basimick and bowed slightly to the woman at the gate.

"I suppose you aren't late still," she attempted to say politely; though Basimick knew she was only doing so because there would be witnesses. "Who have you brought with you to town, Basimick?"

He was eager to tell his sister but was quickly silenced by the shorter of the two who answered for him instead. "Official Imperial business," he said. He cupped Basimick's shoulder and pulled him close. "Wouldn't want to cause a scare," he whispered.

Basimick nodded. "At the town center where the roads meet, there is a stone building where the priest would be happy to help you get some proper rest."

"Thank you, Basimick. The Empire could use strong young masters such as yourself." They began down Mainroad, bowed their heads to Tera as they passed her, and entered through the gate. "We will be gone in the morning and will do so quietly. We hope we caused no trouble, miss."

Tera remained silent as they went by and waited for Basimick to be alone with her. "The medicine?"

"I have it all here with me."

"Very good," she said, correcting her posture to a polite stature. "I was sent by Father to come and get you."

"Was he worried?"

"I think he was tired of me more than anything. Without your banter I fear my wisdom is simply more glum than he'd prefer."

"The price for your intellect, sister."

Tera began home, "If only we were all as well read." They wandered away from town and twilight became night in the woods quickly. As Basimick gathered the medicine from deep in a protected satchel pocket his sister finally spoke, "Who were they?"

"Hunters. Professional Imperial hunters."

"I don't think many fugitives would risk coming into Bassar's region."

"They aren't bounty hunters if that's what you meant, and they were more official than criminal poachers if *that* was what you meant." Basimick smiled as he inspected the medicines to see if he could remember what color matched the proper use.

"You seem a bit too excited for them to be hunting trophy deer, brother."

"Dragons," he tried to whisper but his sister was right about his excitement and he more so shouted it.

"Here?" Her voice did not seem excited and her face turned pale with worry. She was scared.

"A big one they said," Basimick said with less enthusiasm. "I think it might be the reason that the mountain bear came down into the woods that day."

"It's in the Ash Mountains?"

"They think so. They've followed it here from the Badlands."

"You seem too excited, Basimick. Don't be reckless."

Basimick rolled his eyes and turned away from his sister as they walked, preparing for another lecture about his youth and immaturity.

As soon as they entered the house Tera uncovered her father from his blankets. "You have been away from duty for too long," She said.

"Held prisoner by a loving daughter," He laughed. "I have more excuses to leave my post than the dead. Why do you bother me with duty now?"

"Basimick found Imperial dragon hunters in the Ash Wood."

"Don't cause a panic," Basimick said, stoking the fire back to life.

"The mere mention is enough to do so," Bassar said sternly. "Is this true, boy?"

"It is. They say it might be in the mountains."

"I would leave and go far from here if my legs would let me."

"Why? The Empire isn't so incompetent." Basimick thought for a long moment and turned back to face his father, "Is it?"

Bassar turned away from Basimick and looked at his daughter, "The medicine?"

She pointed to Basimick who carefully handed the vials over to his sister. She looked them over as he explained the meaning of each color. She began helping her father as soon as she was sure what the medicines would do and what order to do them in.

"She is old enough to remember, my sweet Tera. You, Basimick, were not yet talking when we left home to come here." Bassar winced as the bandages around his wound came undone. "I speak very little of it, for it pains my heart, Basimick. I think it best you know now where we are from." He began to speak and his children listened...

*****

Bassar stood to the right of the Lord Havvel's throne that rested before a great crowd that had gathered in the forum room where their chatter was near deafening. It was the final days of the Emperor's Tournament, an annual tradition for the city that came during the Flori Festival to welcome in the beginning of Spring. Business had of course drawn the Emperor away as it always had, but Lord Havvel was one of the few who could host such celebrations on the Emperor's behalf.

Havvel leaned over the arm of his throne toward his captain of the guard, "Will you honor him, Bassar?"

"My Liege?"

"A Champion of the Tournaments will receive my blessings of course, but that shall happen the day after next. This is time now to honor the day's victory. Today was swordsmanship and you by right are the best in the land, Captain Bassar. I believe that you had taken the title a few years back now."

"Quite a few years, sire."

"Would you honor today's champion?"

"Yes," Bassar paused to smile. "Yes, of course, my Lord."

"Then come, accept my station's sword and honor them properly." The locals within the crowd knew of Bassar's reputation and clapped the champion of the day on the back to make sure that they also knew what respect they had just received.

Bassar stepped forward, ceremoniously cornered his steps in front of the throne, and knelt down before Lord Havvel to properly accept a most ornate sword. With both hands he took the blade and rose to approach the day's champion. "With the honor of the Lord Havvel, and with the honor I assume, I name thee, Sword Champion." He tapped the sword on each shoulder slowly to draw out the silence of the crowd just a little longer. "May you rise and be recognized for your honors."

As the warrior rose the crowd began to applaud and the bells began to ring in all the towers. Many cheered louder, thinking the bells were part of the celebrations. Bassar seized the moment of distraction and signaled to the Lord Havvel for their departure. Quietly they left by way of a rear door hidden behind the throne and quickly they closed it behind themselves before anyone had noticed. "Bassar, why was the signal raised?"

"I am not sure, my Lord."

They moved quickly through the secret castle passage and arrived at a heavily reinforced door that Bassar eagerly opened for his Lord Havvel. In the next chamber were several armed guards who waited for the captain to give their next orders. Bassar faced one of them, hopeful for answers, "What is it then? Out with what news you all have."

"A dragon approaches from the east. It is an elder beast whose air is of fire, my captain."

"How distant?"

"Near the Gray Wall perhaps, spans away, but by flight we don't know how long."

Bassar looked worried, "Take the Lord and begin alerting the city at the street. They will not understand the trumpets of warning for the fair," he waved off the guards and they rushed away as soon as the order was given. Bassar turned to acknowledge Lord Havvel, "We may yet save the city, my Lord."

Lord Havvel nodded, worried at the coming carnage to his city, and he was led by two guards through another door to stay safe deeper in his keep. The other guards who were within the chamber took haste toward the exits and protected the doorways from any panicked or curious folk. Bassar thanked each of them as they passed and they stood as dutiful statues at their posts. As the door into the inner keep finally shut behind the Lord Havvel, Bassar left through his own passage, toward his own concerns. He left the castle, passed through the western gate, and made quick time to the city docks below the sea cliffs. Throughout the city, the sound of trumpets still called for emergency but they made no difference with the conflicting noise of the festival. No one was yet in panic and he arrived at his home before the bells of the church in his district rang or the sound of fearful wailing rose up in the streets. "Tilde, sweetheart, grab the little ones and come. We must leave the city at once."

His wife took up the baby and then rushed Tera to her father. He caught her under the arms, heaved her onto his hip, and hugged her into a strong embrace. Tilde was quick and listened without hesitation, but she could not help but ask, "What is it, Bassar?"

"Dragon," he whispered to hide it from the children. "And it is a dangerous one at that." Bassar lifted Tera into a more comfortable position and they went into the streets where crowds had begun to mob in the chaos. "Come now," he took Tilde's hand and began to head down the street stairs away from the sea cliff toward the docks in the bay with haste.

As they drew near to the waters they noticed that there were many ships that had already departed from the harbor. Tilde could see a few still that were taking on more of the massing crowds but Bassar turned away from the docks and continued up the shoreline. He was at a fast pace until they were off the paved waterfront streets and were walking along the rocky beaches beyond the harbors. As they got a distance away the first torrent erupted and all at once the sky turned dark with smoke. The awful golden glow of a massive blaze in the clouds lit their way as the sun became hidden. In the bay the great beast stirred the waters under its great wings but the fire from within its maw swallowed ships and sails as the boats rocked to tipping in the harsh waves.

"Close your eyes and stay silent," Bassar said as calmly as his shaken voice could allow. They were alone on the shore but still the screams of the crowded city could be heard, the violence of it all stinging in their ears. The shadow of the dragon swept round and round as the hiss of fire poured out from within.

Suddenly there was an awful crack as the earth itself shook. Above them on the cliffs, where the city rested overlooking the docks that lay on the shores of the bay, the tower keep of Havvelon broke free of its very foundation. It fell as a giant sledge through the neighboring buildings until the top most ramparts fell over the sea wall and bricks began to fall into the waterfront. Hot ash, smoke, and debris fell across their hidden shore and Bassar took Tera to hold below him as stone bricks struck the plates of his armor across his back. He fought through the pain and braced for the impacts as best he could, praying all the while that Christianna or even Aurora herself could come to save them.

As the noise and echoes faded away, and the splashing waves subsided into quiet, the sound of their youngest crying out caught Bassar's attention. "Do not open your eyes, Tera." He left her for only a moment and when he came back he gave to his daughter her brother who became quiet as she took him up. "Keep him safe always, Tera. Follow me now and save your questions for another time." He nodded to her and she nodded back, understanding that there would be time later to wonder.

Together the three escaped Havvel along the shoreline and headed northward, leading with them a few that had survived, away from the darkening smoke and the glow of fire.

*****

Basimick moved slowly to sit before his father who was still and silent in the rocking chair. "Why have you waited all these years to tell me this now, father?"

"It troubles me greatly," He answered quickly. "I left my post and Lord Havvel fell to the dragon Olag who also took away the fairest city in all the Empire. I came here in my own exile of sorts. I am ashamed of what I have done and all my years of service are laughable should I be discovered for the coward I was."

"You were a great and respectable man. You still are. What you do for the people of Kurrum-"

"I do these things because of the debt I owe to so many more. I will never repay that debt. You owe your very life to that debt."

Basimick prepared to protest again but his sister glared fiercely from her post at her father's leg. "Please, Basimick, quiet yourself."

Basimick was silenced, but his mind was racing. Before him were two strangers nearly driven to tears by phantoms of a past he could not imagine. The room was silent for a long while save for the crackling fire.

"Basimick," his father asked for his attention. "I know you must think little of honor at your age, but it is the most important thing you have. It is your goodness, your reputation, and it is all of who you are." Bassar put his hand on Tera's shoulder, "Please, as we ache together, get the sword and bring it here to me."

Tera stood up and wiped her eyes of old memories. She went into the next room and brought back her father's sword. It was broad, made of shimmering steel, and was so ornate around the hilt it must have been forged by a master of the craft. Bassar gently took the blade from her and she returned to mending his wounds.

"This is the sword that I accidently took when we fled the city. It was Lord Havvel's blade. I was using it to honor the day's champion when the alarm sounded. This sword has served as a symbol of my station here in Kurrum and has also reminded me every day of that terror that forced me away from my duty." Bassar took a deep breath, "I want you to use it for a time, take my place and work under my direction."

Basimick was silent but his eyes were wide. *His father's sword.* He reached out and the tips of his fingers met the cold metal hilt. As he began to lift it away Bassar gripped the hilt and blade fiercely, "With honor you would take this blade."

Basimick met his father's eyes and they showed no laughter or thought of silliness. "I would take it with honor, father."

"Good," Bassar allowed himself a slight smile. "And you would do the duty of my position then, knowing that I would know what is best for Kurrum and its people?"

"I would."

"Then you would rid the town of our dragon hunting guests? It is too dangerous to attempt a hunt like this inside and around our borders. Ask that they follow it out and mind the cities. If they could push it eastward to the Badlands I would prefer it. A dragon is nothing to joke about, understanding that they are professional hunters in their own right."

"But what if they were able to slay it here? It could save countless-"

"I would not dare take such a risk!"

"Father, we could slay a dragon and protect much more than-"

Bassar became stern once more. "Do as I have commanded and mind the dark. We must ensure everyone's safety in Kurrum now."

Basimick was bitter inside but kept a stoic face at his time of duty. He fixed the sword and sheath to his belt. "As you command, my captain." Basimick took up the lantern hung near the doorway and lit it with a match from the hearth. As it came to a full glow he opened the door and went into the dark.

Before he was able to cross the yard his sister followed out of the door. "Do as he asks, Basimick," She said coldly.

"I have already put my duty and my honor on it."

"Then say it like you have some, not like you are pretending to know what any of it means."

"I am not in a noble's house or in a place of pride. From what he just said I should be living in the Badlands and eating with the orc." He felt himself become mad at her scolding him again and without a thought he said, "Maybe that bear wasn't running from a dragon, maybe it was just chasing down a failed watch captain for his last bit of tarnished honor."

Tera replaced her sadness with rage and couldn't help but shout, "He didn't leave because of his lord! He left because of his wife! His pride was with us and her!"

Basimick waved her away, "Let me go deal with this. I do not wish to stay in despair over things I was too young to remember."

"Curse you then to repeat it all. Your honor tested wouldn't stand in the shadow of an exile. Be gone!"

With that Basimick crossed the wood bridge and thought about honor, duty, and his life. He was heated and bitter now. His walk in the dark seemed longer than normal and it gave him time to contemplate his sister's words. *Be gone,* it repeated over and over in his head.

He finally arrived at the west gate, closed for the night, and above on the platform where his father should have been was an empty seat. He opened the gate himself with a twist of a simple lever and shuffled inside where he closed it behind him. Down Mainroad were sets of torches that lit parts of the town in flickers of yellow light and he followed them to Crossroad where the cart of the dragon hunters rested near the corner of the stone building on the southern and eastern corner of the Midway. Basimick entered and found the short one, the tall one, Monice, Marccus, and the town bishop in a full conversation about everyone's past endeavors as though they all knew one another.

"Sorry to interrupt," Basimick spoke loudly to no one in particular. "By order of the captain of the watch, you have been asked to leave the village of Kurrum immediately."

"No offense to you, young master," the short one started. "We are tired and mean no trouble. I'd hate to pull rank or writ, but," his voice trailed off as he went for the documents.

"What if I helped you then?"

"Helped us?" The short one looked at the tall one and they both nodded. They could certainly use the extra hands and to leave a night early in exchange for the help wasn't a steep price. "We might be able to use your help, young master."

Basimick smiled, "Then on my honor, as charged by the captain of the watch, it is my duty to help you."

Marccus and Monice exchanged looks as the bishop attempted to protest Basimick's generosity. The appointed guard of Kurrum held his hand up to them and they were all silenced. The short man nodded to his partner and the tall one nodded back in agreement to whatever secrets they had passed between each other. Then the short one reached out his hand and drew the young guardsman into a strong handshake. "Welcome to official business, Master Basimick of Kurrum."

CHAPTER IX
THE RED CIRCUS ARRIVES

The village was hypnotized by the coming of the caravan. Not much ever came to Twin Bridges, a small human settlement that had made a loose agreement with the nearby elves after they began building outside of their woodland border, but on this day there was a colorful arrangement of carriages pulled by all manner of beasts including a pair of rare horses that are seldom seen in the Imperial lands. Excited children were held back from running toward the strangers who were dancing around and between the carriages as they wandered through the village. There were others driving the carts while yet more members of the caravan were atop the roofs of the carriages, inviting the denizens to come see what they had brought.

There were many carriages and the rear of the caravan was still crossing the low stone bridge over a placid portion of the north river while the head of the chain of visitors crossed the second bridge over the south river. Each new carriage brought with it new entertainment for the villagers to see and they quickly summoned more denizens to crowd around the parade. People were no longer worried of being invaded or attacked, but many were instead clapping and laughing with the strangers, following them near to the edge of their village.

As the last one crossed the second bridge out of the village of Twin Bridges the people crowded to see where they were going off to. They murmured to each other, worried that if the caravan went any further the elves would become upset and destroy the colorful visitors. The head carriage made a sharp turn into a clearing within view and the rest of the caravan followed in unison to make half a wide circle against the very edge of the woods where hopefully no trespass had been made.

When the carriages were pushed into their proper places and the crowd of circus youth began pulling tools out from their compartments, the villagers began to cross the bridge slowly. In the wide clearing the shovels began tearing into the dirt. Long metal cylinders were then dragged out from the carts and rolled into a line to make a segmented pole across the open space which aimed at the hole being dug out. With many strong assistants the rings came together and were pinned into place with special rivets.

The villagers were accustomed to work, but what the strangers had built was so foreign that it captivated their attention and dragged them closer to the clearing. Many of the villagers gasped and shouted as a cloud of smoke erupted beside them. Several within the crowd laughed, claiming they had not been scared, though they were teased by the others who had seen them flinch. From the smoke came two young strangers who were garbed in red colored leathers and had red face paint covering them in stylings far beyond the Empire.

"May we invite you closer," the woman said.

"May we tempt you to see it first hand," the man said.

The villagers were unsure of the invitation, but the children of the village were shouting to go with the two who had appeared from thin air.

The man began to juggle several glass stones that caught the light of the sun and sent rainbows over the ground. "We are here to entertain you and show you the wild things of the world."

She began to dance and from her pocket came several orbs that caught fire in the daylight. She tossed them to her companion who began to juggle them, playing now that he needed to pay closer attention to them to stay safe. "Our friend is going to be raising our tent should you wish us to stay for a moment. It is our most favorite time."

The villagers were transfixed by their performance and several shrugged the warnings of others to pass into the clearing to see for themselves what had come to their small little village.

She began to dance around him like a Flori Day pole and a chain was sneaking out from her satchel around him. He began to struggle to keep the flaming orbs aloft and as the chain snuck around his arms the villagers who were *not afraid* flinched. The flaming orbs fell in an orderly straight line directly to his head. As they struck they erupted with a crack into a cloud of smoke where they both suddenly vanished. As the smoke dissipated the clearing was ahead of the crowd in plain view. All the strangers were dressed in red clothes and wore red paint on their faces, each one waving for them to come closer.

The villagers gathered into a crowd and were asked to form into a ring around the area. Some of the young workers then walked a number of spaces from the large hole and threw several spikes into the dirt to mark the edge of their performance. Another cloud of smoke burst from the hole dug a full height down and with a great deal of humor the two emerged from within it, both coughing from their own trick. As they got to their feet he seemed shocked, "The pole is rebuilt!"

"But it's still down. We can't be having this."

The man pointed to one of his companions near the carriage, "Where is Mebruk?" After they shrugged he pointed to another who also shrugged. The man then pointed at someone in the crowd from the village, "Have you seen Mebruk the Mighty?"

They shook their heads but then a loud voice rose over from behind the line of carriages. "Has they called for me?"

He emerged from behind the caravan and the crowd was stunned to see him. He was a giant specimen of a man, the tallest among anyone there and none could claim to even be over the height of his shoulders. The mighty man stretched his massive muscles for a moment and then removed his loose white shirt with well-rehearsed showmanship. He began to cheer and shout for what he was meant to do and the crowd began to chant with him, "The hoist, the hoist!"

All his gathered companions began to cheer along with them for the hoist, calling on the mighty Mebruk to aid them once again. Mebruk posed and made a theatrical display of his strength by moving large stones within the clearing nearer to the pit so that they could be used to anchor the pole in place. As he did his companions attempted to move the heavy metal pole but none were able to roll it or displace it in the slightest.

Mebruk, done with moving stones, then began to pick up the others who were trying to lift the pole and he set them aside as though they were children to him. He lifted his arms and looked at the crowd with a grin. "Come; tell me that you wish to see it. Tell Mebruk you want him to heave the pole, yes." He pointed at a young child whose parents pulled them close with a bit of worry. Mebruk approached them with a large smile and took a knee to appear more friendly. "Can you tell them, young one, for the young ones do not lie, that this pole is so heavy?"

The child looked up to their father who hesitantly released his grip on their shoulder and then they went to the tip of the pole to test it. It was heavy and the child neared fainting attempting to move it at all. Mebruk laughed, heaved the child up, placed them onto his shoulder, and then walked him back to his parents who now laughed along with the crowd.

"Heavy?"

The child nodded.

"Watch! I will show you all now my strength, yes. It will be my pleasure." Mebruk grabbed the tip of the pole and lifted the great metal beam over his head. He began to shove the pole into the hole and when it became wedged he walked along the length of the heavy beam and stood it upright without a hint of struggle.

"Mighty Mebruk," the crowd shouted, "The pole is slanted! The pole will fall!"

"No!" Mebruk laughed and gave a great hug to the pole. "It shall not make Mebruk the fool!" He lifted the entire pole out from the depth of the pit and aligned it properly before letting it drop back into the earth. The ground shook as the pole slammed into the ground and the crowd gave excited shouts as the show gave them a proper fright. "Is good?"

A companion went to the pole and measured it with an interesting tool that was likely more for the show than for actual measuring. "It is right again, Mebruk!"

The crowd cheered and suddenly the companions of the powerful Mebruk brought a great red canvas out from one of the many carriages. They danced and fluttered the canvas so that it dazzled the crowd and as the red canvas fully encircled the pole the crowd cheered. With another display of entertaining skill, ropes were thrown up and around the pole, looped through brackets in the canvas, and then the companions hoisted it into the air. Within moments a red pavilion of incredible size was made, anchored, and opened by a large overlapping door flap.

A man who had not been seen yet by the crowd stepped out, as though he had appeared only with the raising of the tent. He was tall as well, though not above the shoulders of Mebruk, and he dressed in regal clothing of a proper noble status. He bowed before the crowd, "Hello Twin Bridges, village of the Twin Rivers!"

They applauded the efforts of the man who had already done well to steal the town from their daily duties.

"I am Ulric Reddon, and this is the Red Circus! We travel the lands of Nhearn and seek out the talented to bring you the incredible things that this wild time of ours can show you!" He waved his hand and one of the many tent makers began to do acrobatic feats without use of rope or partner. "We have come to entertain you," he waved again and a sudden blast of fire came from the mouth of another participant. "We have come to make you ask the question: how are such things possible!" Suddenly there was someone atop the pole above the tent and they exploded with confetti to suddenly leap out from the crowd as though magic had sent them instantaneously through the air.

One of the citizens of the village, a man with a hat constructed in an official manner and kept clean with indoor activities, stepped forward to Ulric. "We are happy you have come, and it is a better thing to see than another day of labor," his people laughed with the truth. "But we aren't able to offer much to you. We are lucky to have what we do, but sovereigns aren't an easy thing to come by out here."

"No sovereigns required," Ulric smiled and waved his hands wide to invite them. "I did not leave the borders of Imperial lands and come here to your village hoping for sovereigns. I was hoping to share with you my collection of entertainers and break the monotony of your everyday life."

The town elder looked to his people who were smiling with the excitement of a show. "Well then, maybe we could at least feed you."

"We would be delighted for some fresh food. Trail rations and dried meats from the northern territories wear on the soul. Come, come everyone. See what wonders I have to share." Ulric held the canvas open and waved the crowd inside of the pavilion tent.

Inside were seats that had appeared from nowhere, there were many props littered around the edge of the tent, and in the center was a pit of sand that had not been present in the forest clearing before. Even the large metal pole that held the tent aloft wasn't present inside; it was as though the tent was held by magic. From red colored jesters came light inside the tent, each of them holding pole torches that shined like incredible sparkling candles.

The villagers gasped and whispered to each other as new things were discovered around the tent. They all took seats, perfectly enough for everyone to have a comfortable spot, and they were hushed as the lights dimmed from the torches. Ulric then raised a torch in the center ring and he smiled. "Be amazed, and enjoy. You have all in your own way earned such a viewing and I am sure that you have deserved to be properly entertained for some time. I present to you the tamer of the great grass panther, an elf of the plains in the heart of Midland, and his companion who can take down even the wyrmling bats of the northern Terrors beyond the mountains of Dor."

Suddenly the torch was out and Ulric was gone. From the rear of the tent came a great cat that appeared as dangerous in the tent as it would in the tall grasses of its home. The show went on, each presentation capturing the attention of the villagers, and not one was disappointing nor did any out stage another. Ulric watched as his exhibits were able to capture the attention of all within the crowd and he himself was caught up in the enchantment of the show as someone arrived at the door of the tent behind him.

"Master Reddon," she pulled on his sleeve. "I am Kalara of the Twin River Woods, of the wood elves who live nearest to the Forbidden Lands. My people have been called away to the heartland but I chose to stay and now I am all alone to wander my own paths."

"I am sorry to hear that," he said plainly.

"I do not believe I am welcome back if I should find them," she continued. "I think I made a choice not to join something and now I have no home to return to."

"Sorry," Ulric continued to say without commitment to the visitor.

"I have skills though, and I would very much like to travel with you if you'd allow it."

He then became increasingly interested. "You are not from the village here; you are a wood elf, abandoned by your people. How old are you? Couldn't be much older than two centuries," he eyed the girl with suspicion.

"I am only eighty two, and I have not been out of my forest ever before. I have skills that I might use in your show though. I can do tasks and chores to help also."

He pointed to the crowd who were all distracted by the show, "If you can do that, you can come." Joy was forced upon all their faces with excitement that the fire breather summoned with a ferocious roar. Ulric leaned over to whisper to the elf as the crowd gasped under the heat of another inferno, "What do you need to do that to them?"

She began talking and Ulric waved to someone outside of the tent near his carriage. "Lin," he called and waited for him to come near so he could speak softly. "This is Kalara and she is hoping to join, but she needs an act."

"Is this why-"

But Ulric interrupted the thought and nodded to answer the suspected question quietly. "Let us see if we have a newcomer."

As the show came to an end Ulric wandered to the center ring and took a bow that was met with a standing ovation. The elder of the village prepared to walk up and shake his hand but Ulric halted him, "There is one more, if I may. I have not seen this performer, so I do not know what to expect. I do hope that this showing will result in a welcoming of a new addition to our team, however." Ulric shook his head at the elder who seemed anxious that it might be one of the village children. "Allow me to welcome, as the final act of our visit today, Kalara, the elven sky walker."

The lights vanished and up in the highest places of the pavilion, higher than people remembered the ceiling to have been, was a young wood elf who stood upon the narrow end of a long pole. Mebruk held it straight but all eyes were on her. She held two torches that glowed with a white sparkle so that all else seemed dark. The faces of the crowd grew worried for the newcomer and she took that moment to leap from the pole toward the ground. Gasps and shouts filled the air of the tent. One of the torches fell all the way down to the ground where it was then extinguished in the sand.

Most eyes followed the horrific descent of the light and waited for a crash, but several heights above was the elven girl with a single torch to show the way back to hope. She had landed in the dark upon a rope pulled tight by several jesters of the circus, still a dangerous height from the sand. She tested their endurance by bouncing upon the rope and when she was confident she took several steps forward and fell. With only one hand she grabbed the rope and swung herself around. Then, with one leg she maneuvered across the rope. To follow that she caught herself again with only one arm. The crowd was mesmerized by the display and when she neared the end of the rope she effortlessly returned to standing upon the top of it. She threw the torch up and the villagers could not find her outside of its fierce glow, but as it began to fall on the far side of the pavilion she was suddenly upon the other side of the rope to catch it. The crowd cheered, for they had been worried. Kalara made several tumbles to get to the middle of the rope and she sat down. The two who held it tight then began to lower her to the ground and she swung back and forth until the sand caught her.

Ulric smiled as the light returned to the tent and he took her under one arm. "What do the people think?" They cheered, clapped, and stood to praise the brave rope walker. "Seems she is a very welcomed addition. So it is," Ulric shook her hand and leaned in close, "Welcome to the family."

CHAPTER X
AGNITHIA GATHERS

Agnithia Witch-Heart stood upon the top platform of a tower built over an ancient elven border stone that had stood for an Age at the edge of the tree line of the Sentinel Woods. She wore dark armor made from ore discovered deep in the caves beneath her woodlands, at her waist was a dagger twisted with a vile inscription of Maribel, and fixed to her face was a metal mask that concealed her true identity. Despite the mask denying her natural senses completely, she still moved to witness her gathering forces as though her vision was not impaired, as though a boon of magic had granted sight through the metal plate.

From the east, within the oldest portion of her woodland domain, Agnithia had drained all her warriors and even those considered youthful were brought forth. Beneath banners of black the Sentinel Woods were emptied entirely and atop her perch she could gaze over the encampments being formed about her in the grassy fields beside their woodland home. The dark forest curved southward to hug the coastline of the Inland Sea, but she could see far into the distance still, and about the gentle hills were the lights of more camps gathering along the tree line as the wood elves of the Sentinel Woods were summoned to war.

Beneath her arrived a practitioner of the dark moon, an elf whose flesh was coated in pitch and their attire was dyed as black as could be produced. They wore silver embellishments in crescent shape and hosted an obsidian totem about their neck to placate the goddess of the new moon. The moon shaeman rose around the circular stair which spiraled around the ancient stone to a deck where elven lieutenants were meeting to suggest strategy in the upcoming battles. As the shaeman neared them they bowed, silencing themselves to respect the presence of their religious leadership. The shaeman ignored them all and departed the gathering to ascend the stairs to the very topmost platform where the queen of their elvenwood waited.

"The White Queen has accepted our offer to join with the other elven kingdoms in war," the dark shaeman uttered as they arrived at the height.

"Good," Agnithia hissed from beneath the metal mask. "Has she taken the root?"

"She has," they nodded. "Our ambassador has made sure the queen is able to use it."

"That one will be quick to know its purpose. I hope you have not offended her with lower lessons of magic." Agnithia turned away from the view around her and looked at the priest who revealed a box from hiding.

Agnithia reached into the box and collected a polished gnarled stick from within. It had been hewn from the sacred glades deep within the Sentinel Wood and it shared a mystical tether to a piece split from the same tree, the owner of which was far from this tower. "We are ready to march," Agnithia spoke to the gnarl. "We shall await your order."

Agnithia gripped the polished wood gnarl in one hand before turning away from the priest to look out over the growing elven horde again. She waited for only a moment when Queen Hissilanda the White spoke as though she were there in the tower to bear witness to the massing forces as well. The grain of the wood within the gnarl appeared to swirl about as it resonated with power. Agnithia held tight to the magical conduit as a message came directly passed her ears into her head, giving her a vision that the queen was beside her as they spoke together. The dark moon shaeman shied away as a presence of white light arrived at the tower and they retreated to the lieutenants below.

"Prepared so quickly," the White Queen seemed pleased. "Make sure that any additional resources you have are made ready. There are more who will arrive at your border shortly, for I have gained allegiance with the elves in the Twin Rivers glade lands. They shall join with you from the road into the Forbidden Lands before you march."

"We will make sure our warriors offer what is needed to them, my queen."

"I have also gained soldiers from the nomads of the grasses, and I have called on the old oaths of the plain tribes of Aelum'Hau. They shall be sending all their warriors to you, Witch-Heart."

Agnithia nodded, knowing that the queen still disapproved of her cult title. "They will get what is needed."

"When they are ready, you will lead them."

"All of them? What of Bilennia?"

Hissilanda did not hesitate to say, "She does not see the world as we do. She is blind now to greater things."

"Then I shall see it done," Agnithia happily agreed. Queen Hissilanda the White prepared to leave, her grip upon the gnarl waning, and Agnithia Witch-Heart nervously asked, "Are we welcomed to return to the elven home, my queen?"

"Your alliance to that evil god is what has twisted your woods into a withered den of snag and briar," she returned with disdain. "Your corruption was like a disease that would spread to fell all the trees until Vanessa was so saddened that the Fey Wilde itself would shut away from Nhearn forever. Your allegiance to that evil makes our people's victory over Sult worthless." She paused briefly, "It is all worthless now."

"Then it is true?"

"Your god of shadow knows many things. No dwarf is to escape this fate. Your dark priests will find all of them surely. You shall make sure of this."

"None shall be able to hide," Agnithia replied scornfully.

"Perhaps then you might see Krethnarok again, when all this has ended."

"I shall make us worthy of such welcoming. What shall you do?"

"I shall gather more. The far kingdoms of the north have been summoned and bring all loyal to their own battlefields. I expect you to lead your armies and take the first strike upon the dwarves."

"Where is my battlefield, my queen?"

"Go to the dwarven city near your border. There have been no attacks yet and they will greet you without suspicion of your agenda. You shall destroy it absolutely. Make sure that there is nothing left to remind us that the dwarves have ever lived, and when you have done this show the keeper of that place what you have done. Keep the dwarf lord alive until I may share words with them myself."

"I shall keep them for you. Is what you need something I may collect for you?"

"You are to lead the armies and destroy what is asked. Leave further worries for me to contend with."

As the voice faded from her head and the light of her presence faded from the platform the dark moon shaeman returned. Agnithia struggled against a great exhaustion to place the artifact back into its box. "Her presence is overwhelming," the shaeman stated. "She should not have made a light such as that. She should not have had a presence here at all."

"I warned you that she is more than she seems." Agnithia regained herself and looked out over the armies gathering about the border of her woodlands. The storm was still only growing, more elves would arrive, and additional armies still, until none remained in any of the woods or grasslands of Nhearn any longer. "When the other armies arrive we march to the city of Ovelclutch," she ordered from beneath her terrible mask of metal.

"What of our master's plans?"

"It will not take much convincing to attack the dwarven fortress," Agnithia assured. "We will take the peaks of Argenkul for ourselves through the queen's crusade. I would assume that we may complete this and still remain hidden for purpose."

The dark moon shaeman of the deeper woods looked to the tall mountains at the southern coast of the Inland Sea, and even at their distance the shadows of the dwarven spires on the peaks could be seen. "Will we have enough to contend? The secrecy of her cause will last only so long."

"The White Queen assures that the dwarves will not expect an attack," Agnithia whispered. "We will arrive at the gates of Ovelclutch under the guise that we are going to Krethnarok to assist with respite. Hissilanda's armies will come from the west to assist with the Forbidden Lands. When we hear that they have arrived at the gate we shall begin her war."

"Sudden, swift, and absolute," the moon shaeman nodded.

"If any are to escape they will raise alarm and the queen's war will be delayed." Agnithia seemed to stare at the dark shaeman, "Let us not waste this opportunity to act beyond our means. We will see the end of this conflict quickly and return to our plans."

CHAPTER XI
DARK SPIRE

The two Blackroot elves awoke from their encampment before the sun began to rise over the eastern horizon of the Green Bay. Lilium wrapped her face against the harsh wind as the fine white sand of the beach was whipped up in the gale. As her companion woke from the protective pit they had dug for their night on the shoreline she offered another protective scarf. "Better than the wind in the Lowland, Terica?"

"Not as sharp at least. Spent too long in that barren place. Wind was carving the stone apart," she wrapped her face against the grit in the air. "Carved my bones too."

"Seemed more pleasant to take that way," Lilium empathized, testing her own skin for the thousands of scratches they had endured. "Highlands would have had us lost in the moving dunes, or sinking in them."

They buried the pit, concealing any trace that the assassins had rested there. Lilium directed their path back toward the west, away from the gentle waves of the bay, and ahead of them was a valley caught between two sharp ridges of granite that rose to an incredible height spans away where the two mountain spines met together at the westernmost end of the ranges. "What did the library say to do," Lilium asked.

Terica answered but her mood was heavy, "A hidden path will reveal itself with the rising sun. The old High Elves left a secret of some sort."

Lilium squinted into the wind to guess the coming of sunrise but her companion was laden with thought. She had been getting used to having company alongside her, and in a welcoming tone the Blackroot invited the other assassin to speak, "What clouds your mind, sister?"

Terica's eyes shied away, embarrassed that she allowed her thoughts to wander into distractions. "It was last night."

"Restless, but not just last night."

"No," Terica admitted. "Do you think Vanessa is mad with the Blackroot?"

"You would ask if a wolf is upset with its fangs?"

"I haven't had any visions since that day you woke me in Krethnarok. It's all just repeating messages. I have not rested in the Fey, I," Terica hesitated a moment. "I don't even know why we are here, to what end."

Lilium still waited for the sun. "What do you recall from last night's dream?"

"It was dark, I believe I was resting, and then there was shouting in a room beyond my door."

"Do you remember when you were made into a Blackroot." Lilium asked, but Terica shook her head. "What else was there?"

"I remember having my blade," she touched the Blackroot weapon on her hip trying to recall what she had seen in the dream. "As the door opened the darkness was gone, and a white light filled the room, and it blinded me to waking."

"Perhaps it is just your nerves in your dreams."

"Do Blackroot just have dreams?"

Lilium was several centuries older than Terica and had seen many of Vanessa's assassins begin and end. "I have not dreamed, only traveled with her in the Fey Wilde. I do not think that the Blackroot dream."

"Am I," she hesitated to continue.

"No," Lilium rested the statement confidently. "Some get messages differently. Think of the target, perhaps that was your message."

"There wasn't anyone else in the room with me. I have not had a target revealed to me yet. Is that why I am so restless? I just do not know what to see."

"Be mindful, share with me, and I will try to help."

"Do you know what I am seeking?" Terica began to press for an answer from her wise companion, but the east arose in a splendid color, the dawn breaking over the fog gathering in the bay, and Lilium became watchful. They both stared into the valley waiting to see what might be revealed. "Can you see it? Is there a trail?"

"I do, along the southern wall there, marked by a white glare in the sun. The High Elves knew their craft it seems. Any other hour we would be lost."

The pair was quick to travel across the beach toward the valley ahead. With excited haste they arrived at the head of the trail, unmarked except by the hour when High Elves had been clever enough to reveal it and the early sun caught the sheen of the polished mountain rock.

The valley was immense in the morning sun. Before them the mountains rose tall and suddenly as though they were but a sheer wall built by Helena herself. Not once during their time in the Highlands or Lowlands did their desert course expose a way up to the reclusive peaks. Now, on the nameless beaches of the

Green Bay, they found a way into a great valley that split the range into a northern ridge and a southern ridge where distances into their heights rose a solitary peak whose stone was as dark as coal which was stark beside the gray granite of the sentinel spires that guarded it.

Lilium took the first step onto the trail head, "Come sister, I see now where we must go and I fear we may have truly only met the mid of our journey."

"There is no reason we should be here, Lilium." Terica's eyes could see the terrible black mountain ahead of them. "This land has seen shadow and ruin that could not give us clarity now."

"We come to gain wisdom. I can feel it," Lilium smiled and looked into the heights of the mountains with surety. "The High Elves of old would wish us to gain whatever knowledge is left here."

Terica looked to her companion and saw that Lilium was infatuated with the terrible mountain in the depth of the canyon. "High Elves were not known for their dark works," She said. "If what I read in the old texts has offered me any knowledge it was that their works were made with ivory and marble. This place is foreboding and evil. It is not the High Elves like we thought. I wish not to draw any nearer to it." Terica held her head low, embarrassed to have been so excited and then so afraid upon seeing it.

"Terica, you shame yourself. Fearless Blackroot assassin indeed," Lilium laughed. "Come now, join me in what may be our biggest discovery since they left us so many millennia ago. The High Elves have all but vanished and we step now on their threshold merely to turn away?"

Terica seemed displeased with Lilium's bravado, but she could not turn away and leave without further insulting herself. "Then let us be off, before my nerve grows thin again. Lead on, Lilium Blackroot."

They both continued on their way, upward on a narrow ledge that seemed to have been carved hastily in ancient times across the southern edge, cut steeply against the sides of the sheer bare stone. They managed this way for hours and as the sun continued on its path the spire teeth became dark with shadow so that the darkness of the valley crept up quickly. It was only just beyond midday and already there was the haze of twilight behind the western mountains, the shadows of the taller peaks falling into the valley to cast a ward against the daylight.

It appeared to be nightfall when they had reached what the old tome had called *The Bastion*. It rested on a broad ledge, widely carved so that the trail opened up to a tower built on a flat foundation. This tower was built with eight even walls, much as other High Elven structures were claimed to be, and it was built of white marble as the High Elves favorably built from. There was no quarry for it that the assassins could see from the cliff side heights, and the stone looked so alien in the lands where it stood that it must have only been High Elves that brought it from distant territories.

Terica looked over the cliff into the ravine below and hoped Lilium could answer, "What did they hide so far into these dreadful peaks?"

"I wonder if it was something that they fought back," Lilium said quietly. "This fortress tower has no windows to cover our passing through, only those aimed at seeing what comes down from the upper mountains. Do you think," She paused for a moment. "Do you think it may have been the dark knight?"

"The dark knight of Annabel? I do not believe that the legends of that evil had come so far south, nor so far uphill. None of my studies and nothing in that old library would suggest it was Adro'Har," she replied with an air of doubt in her answer. "This place could be hiding anything though," she studied the impenetrable shadows below the cliff.

Lilium shook her head away from distraction and looked at the entrance of the tower where the wood door had rotted into a black scorch upon the threshold. Coming from within were the quiet whistles of the harsh wind hitting the eaves and the smell of mustiness still lingered in the damp halls of the cliff turret. "There is nothing here." She stepped inside, no longer worried of dangerous things lurking within. There was nothing of note, barren but for the loose ocean debris that had been carried in on the wind through the broken rooftop.

"Let us continue on then," Terica hoped not to linger on the ancient cliff trails.

"The way is dangerous and even our Blackroot eyes cannot see the trail so well here. The darkness coming over this place is beyond any I have ever seen, as though the peaks work to keep the light of the sun away."

Terica crept into the tower, "Perhaps a camp here for the night then." She began to jest, "High Elves may watch over us and we could have a fire."

"We still have much of the day left," Lilium pointed through the dark and across the eastern horizon was a hint of dusk and daylight. "I would hate for the spirits to find us napping."

Terica checked the white bricks and touched a few with the tips of her fingers. She smiled a moment with wonder, "There are no spirits out here, only old bones perhaps. We haven't seen any bird or any creature since we first made it into view of these spires. I don't believe that the dead would dare come close either."

As they rested at the Bastion through the evening the sky only became darker, so much so that the brightest stars were barely able to shine through the ominous veil. Beyond, in the bay to the east, the pair of them could see the glimmering light of the early waning day vanishing quickly. "Enough delay then," Lilium took a deep breath to prepare for the rest of the march into the peaks. "Shall we continue? The way narrows ahead."

"When we cannot see the trail," Terica shuttered at the thought.

Lilium squinted into the sky and tried to measure the stars. "When will the moon rise?" They continued to rest within the tower until the moon came over the valley ridge in the south. Lilium peered into the higher cliffs to discern the polished edge of the path ahead. "There, not as well as the morning sun, but once we are upon it we should manage well enough along the glare not to tumble over the edge."

"Lilium, the way out," Terica pointed at the bay but there seemed to be no way of returning to the white sands of the beaches.

In desperation Lilium tried to find the trail again, to see the way out of the Spires, but there was no path. "I cannot see it from here, Terica. There is no trail, or glare, or hint of any pathway down there. Just cliffs and ravines all the way back down. As hidden as when we arrived." She hurriedly moved around to a new vantage, tried to remember where the trail was that led them to the Bastion, but she could not find any evidence of the trailhead. It was as though the trail had simply vanished.

"Perhaps it was made to come in and not to go out," Terica looked up into the deeper peaks of the canyon and there before them was the polished glare of the carved stone trail leading them upward into the darkness beyond.

"Trickery," Lilium said coldly. "A lonesome range of mountains in the midst of nowhere and a trail into them that does not reveal the way out. Whatever is lost here must have been truly terrible to Nhearn."

"The High Elves must have been worried about it. How awful was it to make a prison to keep guard over what is trapped here instead of destroying whatever it was?"

Lilium smirked, "Perhaps they did not ask the Blackroot to take care of it."

Terica was still unsure of what lay in the summits. "We should be on our guard."

"Agreed," and then they were silent for a long while as they stepped onto the trail. It was not hard to follow upward, but they became more aware that with each passing step they could not recall the previous and the way back was lost in a haze of other thoughts. As they neared a rise in the mountains they crossed over a cliff where the two ridges met and the sheer wall defended the dark height from the valley floor. Suddenly the valley had ended and where they stood widened into a great bowl where the peaks made a crown of teeth around a deep caldera. Wind could be seen as the dust of the desert outside of the mountain wall swept up the sharp slopes, over the summits, and through the teeth; but the harsh winds above made the deep pit of rock all the more quiet, and eerily so.

What remained of the day passed by quickly and the moon became more watchful as it drifted over the valley. The pair of them began across the caldera wall and went deeper into the darkness until they could begin to see the silhouette of the great spire in the middle of the sinister pit still shrouded in shadows, even in the direct light of the moon. Upon its peak were the spiral carvings of streets and about it were towers that could be watching them even now.

As they continued around the southern ridge they could now stand side by side and share with one another what at all they could distinguish. The looming spire began to reveal itself as though it chose to shed layers of darkness when they neared.

It was a formation of dark rock that jutted from the caldera wall so that the city built upon it precariously dangled over the very center of the deepest portion of the great pit below. The peninsula of rock had strange towers about it, streets terraced up onto the top mound of the spire structure, and at its peak was the tallest of the foreign towers. All of these buildings were constructed of dark stone, nearly black, the same stone as was deep within the pit. "A city," Lilium questioned in a hushed tone, worried that the wind would carry her whispered words and echo them all the way back to the white beaches. "I was worried it was a tomb."

"Who would say it's not, but worse so. What good is a city with no way out?"

"A fortress?"

Terica pointed around it, "There are no walls-"

"The cliff is the wall."

"There are small dwellings, mismatched streets, there are no weapons either. I do not think this was a fortress."

Lilium looked about at the thinning trail as it made its way to the base of the peninsula of rock on the far side of the caldera. "I guess we shall see when we get there."

As the moon neared the middle of the sky they saw that the pit was still not revealed, even with the silver light beating down from above, the shadow of the jutting rock, the dark spire itself, kept the dark protected within the deep pit.

At last they made it to the city edge where a carved flat plateau was made to build upon, much in the likeness of the flat at the marble tower lower in the canyon. Before them was a gate of polished onyx, a simple stone arch absent from a wall. There had once been a door there but it had been splintered, charred with flame, and was scattered about the threshold as though a ritual had been done upon the arch. All that remained was the polished black stone arch that marked the border of the ruins ahead and in the keystone at the top of it was a perfectly carved hole, round and angled upward so that it pointed into the night sky.

"Look," Terica grabbed Lilium by the shoulder and pointed through the hole. "It is a sign."

Lilium peered through the hole and from where they stood in front of the gate they could see, perfectly placed, was the full moon in the sky so that it appeared as the sigil of the dreadful archway. "It is a coincidence only," Lilium uttered softly. "How many moons has this place witnessed, and how many more would bear importance greater so than this moon. They would have built it such that a great moon, one with more meaning, would shine through." She leaned away and saw the moon alone in the dark sky, "They wouldn't have planned this for two lonely wood elves, even if nothing else lives in this place."

"Of all the time and at this angle, this very moment at the doorstep to this place."

Lilium knew better than to argue against her comrade's superstition. "It is a full moon at least, sister. That means good luck."

Terica smiled, satisfied by the thought of *good luck*. "Watchful eyes for our passage." They held tight to the blades at their waists, stepped through the threshold, and entered onto the grounds of the dark and ancient ruins.

It was a strange and decrepit place that rose over the mound of the peninsula. Towers, dwellings, and low walls terraced the city so that there were streets above streets and switchbacks carved suddenly, shifting upward and downward in all manner of direction. The city was a labyrinth unto itself.

They both moved as uphill as they could, using sets of decaying staircases to get up onto the streets and platforms above. They turned to look over the path from where they had come and found that they were well above the elevation of the strange archway at the city entrance. They continued through the city but had somehow been led downward into a levy where the city's sludge and filth had gathered in a slow moving stream that fell into the great pit at the very edge of the peninsula. Lilium looked around trying to see where the tallest tower was but could not find it in the shadow. "How could we get so lost by moving uphill?"

"This place is so strange, Lilium. We need to keep our wits." They retreated back uphill, attempting once again to recollect their steps but the streets manifested differently. Turns they had thought they made were now unfamiliar, places that were bare stone were now filled with dense mosses, and places that were broken had suddenly been repaired to their pristine craft. "I do not like this."

"Uphill, but let us not be fooled again." Lilium grabbed hold to a ledge of the street above them and lifted herself up. The street was carved smooth and had a gentle bend that seemed to loop around the city with an incline nearing the top of the mount. "Perhaps this way?"

"I doubt it," Terica said in an honest tone. "Be smarter than that, Blackroot. The city is fooling you. This road may just lead a long way back to the front gate."

"You would have us go downhill?"

"If uphill got us to the lowest part of the city, we might as well try."

Lilium did not want to indulge in the strangeness of the weird city, but she felt no need to argue with the logic her companion offered. "Then let us go downhill," she sighed. They started down the street and witnessed statues guarding the way whose appearance was worn by time and consumed by creeping lichen. The buildings became more imposing too, the motif embellishments becoming more haunting as the street began to curve tighter and the grade became steeper. "We are going to be below the tower," Lilium stated.

"I have a good feeling about this," Terica turned around to see where the moon was. It was watching them both from above and she was comforted. The street cornered out of sight suddenly then ended at a large door that was entrenched in the rock so that to either side of the threshold was a smooth unscalable wall. The door itself rested at the base of a sheer rock foundation that went higher and higher until the construction of the city's tallest tower started and higher still was the peak of that dark spire.

"To get to the top, go to the bottom," Lilium shook her head. "The people of this place must have been driven mad, or were perhaps mad to begin with. It is such an odd way to do anything; that up is down, down is up, and there is only ever deeper inward."

"Keep yourself clever now, we go inside," Terica put a finger up to hush.

They both approached the door and were surprised to discover it unlocked. The hinges grinded open and the metal door scratched on the stone floor. There were loose things strewn about in the tower, books and cauldrons tipped over centuries ago. There were plants growing in the streets whose roots had invaded inside, mosses and lichens splotched the walls, and the sound of dripping dew in the empty hallways came to their ears at irregular times.

They entered the rise of the tower, its structure dangerously decrepit, and there were dark bricks collected in piles on the floor after they had come loose from where they had sat in the walls. Fragments of the inner chambers had collapsed making random halls and makeshift doorways throughout the ancient place. The lichen and roots gathered around the stone and gripped the structure near to sundering, though it may have been the only thing keeping the tower intact.

There wasn't any source of light from within the tower, no torch sconce or cauldron blaze, but the damp of the tower still glistened from the broken cracks and windows where moonlight filtered in white rays into the spire. As the shimmer glinted from the edges of the black stone it transformed into a sinister hue. "Ungodly light," Lilium whispered.

"Perhaps you would prefer the dark to creep in," Terica risked saying.

"*Is that so,*" a faint voice whispered in the tower halls. "*What use would you have in the darkness, sylvari?*"

Lilium slid to a wall across from Terica. They looked at each other and Terica stared back with an angry glare. In silent movements of her hands she communicated: You. Said. Nothing. Lived. Here.

With quick gestures of her fingers and tapping of the forehead and nose, Lilium replied: I. Expected. Orc. Maybe. We Are. In. The Badlands. After all.

"*Nothing lives here, sylvari. Though if I do yet live then I have long forgotten the purpose of it.*"

Lilium knew that whatever was ahead of them could read their gestures. Boldly Lilium shouted, "Do you mean us harm or can we speak."

"*If darkness is your companion, step forward. I wouldn't wish harm to a visitor of my keep. Come forth so I might enjoy your company properly, sylvari.*"

Terica crouched and crept forward quietly with skillful steps, "Carefully."

They both moved up a crumbling stair and then through a hallway toward the center of the decrepit tower. The chamber was built so that there were eight walls, each facing the cardinal ways and the crossways in the same fashion of the High Elven Bastion. In the middle of the room where the tile had once been was a hole in the floor that fell away into the darkness below so that even the magical moonlight that glared from the bricks around the tower could not see beyond its depths. At the bottom of the hole could be heard a whispering of the wind, a way out of the tower over the great pit that rested under the precarious foundation of the ruined city.

Above the abyssal pit, entangled through holes throughout the tower, were black vines, a bramble thicket that clung tight to the walls, the ceiling, and around to other anchors beyond the view of the room. Inside the middle of this twisted darkness was a mass that appeared as a pod of sorts and it began to unravel itself. From within the dark vines was revealed a face of beauty and the moonlight from the windows and fractures of the tower became altogether brighter as she appeared.

"Youthful sylvari. I envy it so."

"I am Lilium of the Blackroot. Who are you?"

It spoke with two voices, though the sweeter of them was more audible. *"Lilium, that name seems a familiar sort. I am Lolillith, for I have since forgotten the name given to me at my birth."* The vines tightened a bit as the face entered a space of deeper thought, but she did not appear pained by the struggling vines. She was calm and still for a while as the tendrils of darkness moved and anchored anew to keep her aloft in the tower. Each of the vines became tighter and tighter until they became fully taut. Lolillith rested her eyes and appeared to sleep in the ever tightening bramble.

Lilium held still and Terica whispered to her, "It's sinister. I do not trust it."

"I imagine this must be what we have come for."

Terica shook her head and kept her eyes fixed on the pod. "Then let's do it and be done."

"Afraid?"

"Never," Terica was quick to say, still embarrassed for trying to avoid the mountain trail. "Blackroot know no fear. I am waiting for treachery."

Lilium nodded, knowing that Terica could be wise to such things, but this monster was so ancient she could not trust any feelings for chance. "Lolillith?"

"I apologize. I have not needed to think or bear witness for a long while." Lolillith shivered and the whole tower trembled as the dark tendrils relaxed about her. *"I was there long ago, a progenitor of my people. I had been tricked by sin and darkness into what I am now. What a fool I was in my youth, though even then I must have been many millennia into my prime. My name, I have forgotten, I had taken other titles and moved on from the need to remember such things."* She shivered again and some of the bricks cracked so that dust lifted away from them to drift about in the stagnant air. She closed her eyes once more and went into thought causing another shiver that threw whole bricks from the walls and ceiling.

"Lolillith, do not worry about such ancient things," Lilium offered.

The monster's eyes opened and the dark limbs let go enough that the beautiful face managed a deep breath inward. The limbs of Lolillith's pod became thicker and the breath moved about the tendrils in all directions like the pumping of blood. *"It has been some time, I'd imagine. How is the state of the Eternal Empire that keeps me here?"*

Lilium and Terica glanced at each other but neither had ever heard a whisper of such a thing beyond the tomes of the ancient library.

"So it has been much time then," Lolillith laughed as much as she was able against the suffocating cocoon. *"Victory at last, though it is a bitter history I keep only to myself now."*

"Victory?"

"We were at war for thousands of years. I was once who they were, the High Elves, but I was foolish and had been taken by the darker things in Nhearn. I was made into a Dark Elf, a shadow of myself." The beautiful face struggled some but eventually a tear managed to fall out of its eye. *"I do not remember why I did so now, but I have regret for my entire existence. I have been with such madness for so long I fear it may be all I am now."*

"A shadow of sin," Terica whispered, remembering the old passages that had led them to the Dark Spires.

"What is it," Lilium turned to her companion. "What do you know?"

Hesitant, but urged on by Lilium's intrigue, she stepped toward the bramble. "I know who you are," Terica stood tall before the moonlit face. "I know not when, or about your wars and empires, but I have heard legends of High Elves, and I have read only one mention of Dark Elves. You are Lolillianna. You are the first Dark Elf."

"My name? So close it was, yet my mind could not remember the sounds of it. Did your ancient tomes say how I fell?"

Lilium sat back as Terica came forward. "There are no stories left in Nhearn but for the lone verses that led us here."

"I can recall the memories, though it would not be of merit to you, sylvari. You have traveled far from your heartland. My memory fades, and this may be my final warning to the world."

*****

108

While the hordes of the orc nations were pushed back into the deeper regions of the Badlands and the clans of humanity were corralled into manageable territories, the Eternal Empire of the High Elves grew its dominion further than it had ever done before. The war amongst the gods was lessened during the leadership of the High Elves and a deep breath of peace was felt by all within their lands before further turmoil would surely strike. These few years through the Age of Woe, a time before the Empire of Man had emerged, were documented as a golden era, and much of the evils of Nhearn were purged from within the borders of the Eternal Empire. Himmel, Highborne and first of the High Elves, ruled over the Ivory Cities of the Eternal Empire, and life was well among all their holds.

During a harsh winter, in the course of a new moon, through a celebration of the Noctuni Festival, the coming of winter, during the final days of the month of Deca, It came to the eastern-most border city in the Eternal Empire, the mountain city of Fellus. It arrived atop a dark steed that was adorned with black barding and dark iron plates as though the beast were ready for war. The rider could be seen along the road from a great distance, for in Its left ironclad hand It carried a high banner of black cloth with only a white crescent to claim Its loyalty to the Goddess of Darkness, Maribel, the keeper of the new moon and assistant to the Dark God Annabel. It bore a set of armor in the dark likeness of Its mount made from black iron. Over Its head was a helmet made of obsidian, adorned with a crown of sharp black spikes, and where a face plate should have been was only a pit of dark so absolute that no features of the rider could be witnessed. Although It rode up to the front of the city in the dead of night, the guard at the gatehouse noted that everything became shadow and the stars themselves disappeared as It came upon them. It wore a cloak of purest black that flowed about behind It as a shadow, but a deeper darkness also rode with It. Where It rode the night was touched by something vile that stole the remaining light from around itself.

By strange fascination, or cursed by heavy magics, the guards of the gate allowed the Dark Rider to enter the city through the moon crested arch without question, knowing Aurora would protect them if it meant harm. It moved between the high towers of the High Elven city with a long shadow as Its ally, beckoning the denizens of Fellus from their revelry to follow in throngs behind the heavy clatter of the dark steed's iron hooves on the carven streets. It moved without halt or contest, the mystery of the strange guest tempting the whole city with intrigue. It rode into the city's center forum, a great open square set before the overwhelming heights of the city's fortress keep. It went to the stair that led steeply to the gates of Fellus' keep before any could rebuke the rider. The Dark Rider, still atop the steed, rode up the sharp switchback staircase, rising above the forum plaza to a platform balcony set before the gate of the city's keep where often the lord of Fellus would speak to its people.

From the great height of the oratory It spoke to the gathering elves below, "I come with the blessings of my home to deliver news of your God and of your only path to salvation!"

The reaction of the crowd, which was now more than half of the city, was more curious than fearful of the stranger's words. The throngs below hushed and the silence they allowed only helped the speaker's voice boom deeper into the city. The echoes through the avenues of Fellus summoned those who had retired from the winter festival for the night and even more citizens flocked into the forum below the oratory. News of their Lord God Aurora pulled the attention of any that were left roaming the streets of Fellus, and all of the city gathered below the oratory.

"I arrive now, from a city in the lands of men, far to the west! It was long held by the elves of your Eternal Empire, of Himmel's own kin! Aurora herself resided within the halls of the church there to protect the High Elves residing in the city, and it was there that she had failed to protect against the powers of evil!" The voice carried through the forum, blasted against the walls, and echoed through the avenues of the city. The voice was neither in one moment beauty nor horror, but it boomed so fiercely that all other sounds fell silent. "She was defeated in battle, distracted by her passion of vengeance, her purpose was lost, and beset by shame she has been driven away by Maribel, the true Lady of the Moon!

"Do not fear," The Dark Rider continued, Its voice becoming as gentle as a breeze in the night. "I come to you all with truth, opportunity, and salvation. Between Heaven and Hell, or to your own resting place hereafter, there is no reason to fear inevitability any longer; for she offers purpose to you."

It was expected that war among gods would be difficult and that even Aurora herself would face loss during the many millennia that stretched through the perils of the Age of Woe. Despite any loss already had or yet to come, the High Elves would not so easily forsake their goddess. No one spoke up against It however, and from below the silence that buried the

High Elves was almost as terrible as the Dark Rider's news.

From behind the vile speaker, revealed by the opening of white marble doors of the Lord's Keep, she came to meet It. She wore shining silvered armor with a clean white cape that draped just above the ground without effort. In her hand was a beautiful silvered sword that pointed directly at the heart of the enemy before her very gate. Lord Lolillianna had arrived and her people below braved the silence to cheer as though they had only just realized what danger had befallen them. "How dare you come here and speak as though you were invited." Her guard, a pair of silver clad warriors, armed with wondrously ornate silvered halberds, went to block escape at the stairs as Lolillianna pushed forward to set the Dark Rider against the high balcony cliff of the oratory. "We should take your tongue for what lies you have tried to spread to the faithful."

The Dark Rider met the lord of the city without fear. It did not draw out the strange weapon It bore, nor did It step back in retreat to be pushed over the edge, cast down to the forum below. Instead, It withdrew a small ornate box from somewhere within the dark folds of Its cloak. The box was made of black metals and was only the size of the Dark Rider's palm. Across all of the box's faces was intricate detailing of thorny vines that intertwined chaotically. The only exception of the chaotic vines was its top where a fanged skull rested and bit down upon a keyhole. "This holds the truth yet unspoiled by what you assume are my Lord's lies and answers true to my preaching here. Your God has failed you. You and your kin may yet suffer the same fate as those who followed there unless you heed my coming and ally yourself with the true Lady of the Moon."

With a light toss, as though the tiny box was of little consequence, the dread was passed on to a new victim. Lolillianna called her guard to keep the tips of their pole-blades pointed at the uninvited, but she herself sheathed her weapon and continued on to act in a dignified manner with their guest. She rolled the box about in her hands and locked eyes with the ruby stones set in the hollows of the skull relief. "The key-"

"Is intrigue," the Dark Rider interrupted the thought.

Curiosity driven, the Lord's fingers touched the keyhole and the sound of the pins inside could be plainly heard as though a heavy key had twisted them into place. The elven lord looked at the Dark Rider but could see no hint of gesture, nor could she catch a gaze from within the shadow of its dark helm.

"See truth now and join me to set right the failures of lesser gods."

It was heated anger, an attempt to prove this vile guest wrong, which drove Lolillianna's hand to open the box.

"Lady Lolillianna," called one of the guards after a moment. They witnessed anger move quickly into terrible sadness and she became tearful as the box closed.

"It is true," she replied to them after a long moment of silence. "Aurora has failed. The High Elves have failed. The Dark Rider preaches truth to us."

While the one of the silver guard kept their weapon pointed against the Dark Rider, the other moved to her side and helped her stay upright. "Our Lady, what you claim is heresy. These words, this alignment to the enemy, it is punishable by death. Would you forsake Himmel, the Eternal Empire, even Aurora for this speaker of evil?"

"I would show you this truth if it were not but poison in my heart. I would not wish this knowledge to be shared beyond my own mind and I would surrender it back to this dark speaker if it would not lead me astray from the truth they have brought us."

"What would you ask of us," begged the guard who became saddened alongside their lord.

"If it is true that this dark visitor comes with our salvation, that our own God is no longer capable of deliverance, then it may be that the whole of our Eternal Empire is doomed. Himmel will lead us all to oblivion and our forgiveness will be called on by the mercy of Maribel, perhaps even Anabel herself." Lord Lolillianna lowered to the guest on bended knee and she was followed then by her loyal guards. "What would you request of us?"

The Dark Rider was direct, "Convert your churches, remove from them the silver moon, and accept the truths that the black moon has already laid before you. Expect that you will be challenged by your brethren who are yet unaware of this truth, prepare to battle the misguided of Himmel's empire, and deliver defeat to your enemies with the guidance of your new master."

Many in the grand forum below could not believe such heresy and a murmur of discontent rose in volume throughout the crowd. Disloyalty had yet to occur in all the lands or in all the time of the Eternal Empire and fear of retaliation from Himmel loomed at the forefront of everyone's mind. One in the crowd took a step onto the side of an Auroran statue and called above the crowd to pledge his loyalty to Lolillianna, lord of the city. "We have never surrendered to an enemy and we have always been given true purpose from the Lord of the Keep. May Lolillianna guide us as she always has!"

Yet another rose up and rallied before the steps of Aurora's forum shrine, "What you call loyalty to the Lord of the Keep is heresy to the Eternal Empire! It is temptation given way to the evils of Maribel! May you be judged for your sins against Himmel and Aurora!"

It was strange how quickly the High Elves in the forum joined to a side in the fight. The open plaza below became a violent battleground almost instantaneously. Auroran paladins, practiced knights of the Moon with gifts of holy power, revealed themselves from the crowd and outmatched their opponents with ease, slaying many of the soldiers who cried out their allegiance to the Lord of the Keep. Warriors still loyal to the Eternal Empire began killing those who cried out to the Dark Goddess for safety and the chaos left many dead in the forum. Battle did not end there however, for the violence continued out from the heart of the forum into the city which became lit in the night with riot and flame.

The guards of the keep arrived and news was shared of the new allegiance. They left the protection of the keep and challenged the forces from gaining ground against the lord, resisting the Aurorans as the holy warriors tried to purge the evil that was corrupting their city.

The Dark Rider watched from the oratory balcony as the horror unfolded, never once assuming any would actually brave the stairs to reach them. "This city burns for the moment, but as a flush to a wound, your streets must be purged of the old ways." The Dark Rider turned to speak with Lolillianna who still knelt with fealty. "Let the true Lady of the Moon settle here and guide the faithful to your cause. When the dawn comes we shall call those still living to swear themselves to our new beginning or pass on with their fading beliefs."

Some High Elves of the city who had been protected by the Aurorans had managed to escape from Fellus through ancient avenues and catacombs beneath the foundation. The few survivors that left the pathways below the mountain were asked by the Aurorans to travel back to other regions of the Eternal Empire and send news of the city's fall with them. A storm gathered over the mountain, the clouds of despair returning as the Age of Woe continued on.

The fighting continued throughout the night and many streets were set ablaze with the littered dead. Whole districts were lost to ash, towers that had stood for a thousand years now collapsed to rubble, and shrines that had offered bastions of protection to the faithful became grounds of graffiti and vandalism. Anything that resembled Aurora, or bore a silver moon in her honor, was overtaken by the fervor of the promised salvation. Evil corrupted quickly through Fellus, and in the morning, just as the Dark Rider had ordered, a crowd was gathered before the doors of the desecrated church in the forum plaza, each elf ready to pronounce their loyalty to Maribel.

Lolillianna herself opened the door of the church and the final Auroran of the city held ready to stop her from entering. "You have lost your way," they claimed. "You had led us through millennia, helped save the region from the orc, helped save the good hearted in man, and you saw the building of this fair city to make sure that all our effort of Aurora's purpose was kept. Lord Lolillianna, you were an Auroran as I, chosen by Himmel to found Fellus, to lead us through the dark lands far from home. Do you not see that you have set us against each other, that your warriors and the faithful have slain each other for the words of a twisted messenger? Who has lost their way? Surely it is not I. Turn again to the moonlight. Save yourself."

"There are things that the silver light does not see, and in the shadow of the new moon are stirrings of her failure. She has kept us blind in our zealotry, lied about her ability, and has betrayed even her own purpose. This is the only way to our salvation." She sealed her devotion, proved her worth to the Dark Rider, and with her own blade she overtook the final Auroran of the city of Fellus.

The Dark Rider then entered the church and began the rites of corrupting the silver moon to the dark moon of Maribel. Every High Elf that was left in Fellus came to the Dark Rider, one at a time to the church's sacred moon pool, a placid bath that stretched through the church's main room. It was once filled with clear water and the windows above were carefully carved into the roof so as to let the moonlight shine in rays of silver upon it. This day the waters were as black as a new moon and the pool smelled as though a putrid sickness had settled into it.

Each High Elf passed by the Dark Rider and begged from It, "Please show me the way to salvation."

"Come," It would say gently. "Be healed of your ills and gain the truth I possess."

The ceremony continued as every High Elf, one at a time, entered the pool and waded across it to the altar on the opposite end. Lolillianna herself waited there and greeted each to the new following as they emerged from the dark waters. "Welcome to your salvation," She would say. "Do you understand now what I know to be truth?"

"I have gained truth," They would say before moving on to cleanse the city with their new knowledge pushing them onward.

Everyone worked together, just as High Elves had always done. The city was cleaned, rubble was removed, ash was swept clear, and everything that was of Aurora had been collected into a great pile before the oratory. Not a word was spoken for weeks as the work continued. It was not until the first night of the next full moon that sound once again blessed the city. A great horn sounded and summoned the devoted to the forum where they gathered around a collected pile of old traditions. Above, on the platform of the oratory, were Lolillianna and the Dark Rider to speak from the high balcony.

Lolillianna stepped in front of the Dark Rider and began to speak so all below could hear, "We have accomplished a great task and removed ourselves of burden from a failed God. Let us now show our devotion to the true Lady of the Moon by removing what trinkets we have left through the purification of fire. Let the full moon bear witness to the end of our devotion as we move on and embrace our new lives in the dark of our new Lord. Tonight we shall become perfection. We will no longer be tainted by the passions of a mad Goddess, our lives will instead be led by the gift of freedom now given to us and we will be liberated by the new purpose now bestowed upon us by our new patron. Remove the shackles of Himmel and his Eternal Empire, become new, and find purpose with promises of Maribel." Lolillianna raised her hands and what remained of her royal guard set the pile ablaze with arrows from all around the forum. The crowd raised their hands as the flames rose and they all began to chant in unison as though they had always known the old rituals of Maribel.

The Dark Rider approached the edge of the oratory and silenced them with a wave of Its metal hand after the fire subsided into an even burn. "Be proud that you have chosen this new path, find solace in knowing your salvation has been honored, and wait now for Maribel to come; for she wishes to honor you with her presence. She will come here into her new church and speak to any brave enough to witness her. Prepare for it, she arrives at the coming of the new moon."

The crowd cheered and an excited murmur filled the streets. The Dark Rider spoke quietly then to Lolillianna, "Prepare your masses, they may become afraid of themselves after their change, but reassure them that this is a divine change, and is necessary."

Lolillianna nodded, "What must I do?"

"You will lead the way and become new. You shall be Lolillith, a High Borne risen from the lesser caste."

"Is such a thing possible?"

"It will take time to see that your new master is powerful, but do not ever doubt her."

Lolillianna became afraid of the Dark Rider's words and remained quiet for a time.

"You will then lead your people and conquer the misguided followers of the false God. In only a very short time the Eternal Empire will be met with an unrivaled violence."

Lolillianna nodded.

"More will arrive to you as I depart. You will prepare them to fight and you will prepare your city as a fortress. Your Empire will be born in war and your people will become stronger for their sacrifices."

Lolillianna continued to nod.

"You will be graced soon by your new God, but for now I must leave to fulfill the wishes of my Lord." With that the Dark Rider simply left the city and continued on Its way without a celebration of departure or collection of rations. As mysteriously as the figure arrived It was gone, but the damage was done.

*****

The terror before them shivered once more and Lolillith's eyes closed as her thoughts wandered into antiquity. The decrepit tower shook as the anchors of the heavy bramble tensed. Dust escaped the crevices so that heavy clouds drifted into the rays of moonlight and there was the sound of distant clacking as bricks fell loose from the walls to echo through the empty chambers. Lilium and Terica held still as everything settled back into place and became silent.

Terica waited to speak until the beautiful monster opened its eyes again. "Your warning, what was it that led you astray?"

"*I am not set astray, sylvari, for I am everything that was promised to me.*"

Lilium questioned, "What were we drawn to find here? What was in the black box?"

Lolillith's voice was soft and gentle, but it carried a heavy weight of terrible sadness. "*Now that I have recalled such a memory I would not dare to utter it. What you see before you, this monster, never happened to another of my kin. A Dark Elf does not simply become as I am.*" The tower shook again as she struggled to take a deep breath. "*I am as you see because of the truth that was shared the day I chose my path. Curiosity drew me there, no hand of evil to force me, but I would not offer you such a thing. There is no redemption for me and I am too old to host such regrets as to burden your sin on my shoulders.*"

"Why are you here," Terica asked.

"*Imprisonment,*" Lolillith answered without needing much recollection about it. "*I watched as my city collapsed and all torment of the Gods was done. She did come, and I remember her still. The New Moon, Maribel, the champion of the night, then came and saved what remained of my city. When the mountain itself cracked she smiled at me, and then she hid me by a veil of darkness here. The High Elves feared to come into the mountains again, and no God dared to near these spires. They guarded the way out until only I was left.*"

Lilium then asked, "No God dared?"

"*Not even Aurora,*" Lolillith laughed. As she composed herself she gently grinned and her eyes slowly fell upon them both with all seriousness, "*Why have the sylvari come?*"

"Great need," Lilium stated. "I am a Blackroot, an assassin of Vanessa."

"*An ancient order, perhaps the first of such things. Your God, sylvari, was never afraid to take action. Then it is my weapon that you seek?*"

"Anything that could help. Our oldest libraries have led us here."

"*Well guided you must be, though I sense a greater intervention than you yet realize. Perhaps one younger than I, though which of them would lead you to such ancient wisdom?"*

Terica did not want to offend their host but she refused to have any other take the credit of their successes. "Our own efforts for our own tasks."

"And our task is lofty," Lilium tried to recover from her comrades' potential misstep.

Lolillith did not seem to care or take mind of any commentary that the pair of them had. She instead seemed curious and the beautiful face struggled to smile as its energy began to dwindle from ages of dormancy. *"What is it that Vanessa desires of you, Blackroots?"*

Lilium answered confidently, "I must kill that which cannot be slain."

The anchors shook and the face became more revealed from the terrible bramble as if it were a widening eye that needed to focus upon the visitors. The light within the room became radiant, *"Only a Blackroot could manage such a task."* It smiled widely at Lilium, *"I shall help you."*

Lilium was happily surprised, "You will?"

"A trick," Terica added rationally.

"No trick, sylvari, but my motivation is my own. At rare times the goals of the greater good and the devices of true evil might unite. I too desire your outcome, Blackroot."

"Evil," Terica continued to question.

"Do not misjudge me. I am pained, I have been used, and I am forgotten by all in this world and even myself, but I would not leave my calling, for it is my desire, my own truth. The dangerous path and misunderstood purpose of a Blackroot must understand my struggles."

"How will you help us," Lilium nervously tried to end any fault before the assistance was lost.

Lolillith closed her eyes and the light grew dim within the tower. A black tendril fell from the bramble and went below the floor. It stretched into the hole that traversed the innards of the tower and stretched to an unknown depth. The whistling wind at the bottom ceased for a moment and then began again as the tendril returned to Lolillith. *"I have kept this safe for a long, long while. I wonder what freedom will come to me when you leave here with it."*

The pair waited as the tendril fully returned and in its curled grasp was a dark shard of broken metal affixed to a simple hilt. It resembled a dagger with a razor's edge, formed in a strange black metal that released no glare, sheen, or glint. Across it were markings of evil, script and runes from the vaults of Hell that were legible only to Annabel herself.

Lilium reached to grasp the hilt and it was offered to her freely. Lolillith took another deep breath that sent a pumping motion through the black vines as she sighed. *"With my blessing, take it. This shall complete your task and you shall be the greatest assassin who has ever existed in record and before, at least any that I yet know about."*

"It is evil," Lilium stared at it in her hand.

"It is the most evil, more so than anyone or anything before it or to come after it. Use this wisely, for it has only one use upon it and only one purpose to claim it."

"What purpose is that?"

"It has the power to deal a mortal wound to an immortal being." Lolillith stared at the ancient blade,

taking notice that the moonlight in the room seemed afraid to reveal itself around the dark and wicked thing.

Terica stared at it also, "Why trust us? It can destroy you too."

Lolillith laughed at the threat in spite of the many dark entangling vines strained upon her. "*It would take far less to undo my life and it would betray your purpose to use it here, sylvari. Complete your task, for it is but a small piece of my own.*" The beautiful face slowly disappeared into her dark cocoon with a hideous laughter that echoed in the silent tower so that the second voice lingered in the dark corners until it faded long after the creature had vanished.

"Lolillith?" No answer came. "That must have tired her," Lilium waited a moment to test the monster's sleep. "Very bold, Terica. For one so afraid to come you spoke a great many times."

"I am glad it did not unravel anything. I do not believe it could have been offended by us."

"I was afraid, sister."

Terica smiled, "Fearless Blackroot assassin, indeed."

CHAPTER XII
THE DRAGON

The sun was still not up but the light of the coming dawn had finally pushed away the stars from the dark of night. "Time again, master Basimick," one of the dragon hunters said as he set the cart down and stretched his back before giving the yolk to Basimick who had not slept much in the back of the cart. His excitement was so overwhelming that he could hardly imagine a thought of rest and he pulled the cart eagerly. The yolk was draped over his shoulders and the handles had a comfortable leather grip. The wheels moved easily, greased with fine oil, and even the incline did not hinder the cart in any way. The hunter moved to the back and took Basimick's spot at the edge where they sat and tried to rest before the coming encounter.

When his wit caught up to the daylight he could no longer recognize the forest. It was still the Ash Woods, but it was unlike the woods around Kurrum where the underbrush had been cleared out and controlled. This land was rugged and heavy with overgrown thickets. The gentle foothills where his town resided had passed and become great granite cliffs that were carved apart by narrow streams or had been split by ancient earthquakes. Trees were becoming sparse near a great line across the whole range of the Ash Mountains where altitude no longer permitted them to grow.

"Where was the dragon last seen, Cassius?" Basimick heaved the cart over a rock stuck under its wheel and glanced over to the short fellow who rested on the edge of the cart across from their partner waiting for their next turn under the pulling yolk.

"Longinus, show me the charts again if you could."

The tall one reached into a pack deeper in the cart, pulled out a paper wrinkled by weather, and then began to unfold it with a brute confidence that it could not be torn. "The assumption is that the dragon will find a large cave or a narrow crevice of some kind. So far it has taken to hiding in such places out in the Badlands after it makes its attacks on the Empire."

Basimick couldn't help but ask, "Does this dragon have a name?"

"They call it Olag," Longinus said, still looking at the map of the mountains. "Olag of Fire."

Basimick's heart sank but his desire to see the beast only increased. "Olag," Basimick tried to sound surprised by the name. "Has it been giving the Empire a tough time?"

"Aye," Cassius nodded. "Been working to stop it for a while, near to a few decades. Got the attention of our hunters when it ruined that city back in Southrunn. What was it again?"

"Havvel," Longinus answered. "Been striking little places every now and again, but we've been tracking it this time for nearly a year."

"Had a bit of luck when it passed over Gray Wall on the east side and took a rest there. Dragons rest for a while. Had a few more lads when we tried that time."

As Cassius and Longinus began thanking and paying tribute to the guardsman who had gone with them during that hunt Basimick's mind wandered. This was *the dragon*. It was the one that ruined his family, destroyed the homeland that he knew nothing about, and had disgraced his father. It made him sad to think of such things, but to see the dragon, even get a chance to kill it, was more reason to keep helping the hunters. The Gods must have drawn all of the fates together; made it so he could become a tested man, return the lost honor to his family, and gain the respect of his father in one moment. With new found zeal Basimick continued to pull the cart into the highlands, into the very clouds that got trapped against the sheer walls of the Ash Mountains.

The team of three continued up into the granite slates and came to an ancient pass in the mountain summits. It was the only way in or out of the valley ahead, a desolate place where nothing living grabbed onto the rock or dared to breathe in the silent air. They cast out fear and began into the valley. Within the ravine, between two high walls of stone, they crossed over fields of flaked rock and gentle streams that fell from springs in the peaks above that carved deep gouges through the mountain.

"I admit these mountains are foreign to me," Basimick said quietly to not disturb the stillness of the air.

"I do not blame you. Your woodland seems an absolute paradise compared to this awful place," Longinus answered as he once again brought the map to his face. Cassius cautiously assumed the cart from Basimick while Longinus got the heading, "In my professional opinion, this canyon is the most likely place for a dragon. It has already eaten up a few herds of cattle-"

"And some farmers," Cassius interjected with a mighty heave of the cart. "Gave us a few weeks to find the lair I'd wager."

"But I doubt we are far from it now. I suspect that it would come and rest here in this isolated place," Longinus folded the map and put it back into the cart as Cassius pulled the cart over a final rise. Sure enough, as the hunter's professional opinion had dictated, down below in the narrows of the valley ahead, Basimick spotted the dragon.

The great beast lay before them in a terrible curl of wing and tail nestled within the narrowing chasm of granite. It was a strange and stark contrast as the gray rock was unwilling to hide one scale or hair of the dragon's massive crimson body. Basimick looked upon it with terror and pleasure, for beyond the occasional bear or Auroran pilgrim, he had never before witnessed a more powerful thing in all his life. Legends or myth could not offer any sense of truth to the incredible presence of Olag the dragon.

Across the back of the dragon, from the neck to the tail, were thick scales of a red rusty color that shimmered in the light like fine smithied armor. Along the belly, from its throat to the mid of its long tail, were brighter scales that looked as intense as fresh blood. The dragon's legs were powerful, and at each of three toes were obsidian black talons the length of a grown man. At the shoulders were claws of black, curved for gripping and surely strong enough to sunder the hardest stone. The beast had folded its wings but the violent orange of the membrane could not be hidden away under the long red bones that stretched them.

At the crest of its head and going beyond the shoulder down the spine was a mane of thick black hair that stood upright like quills. It bore likeness to a fine fur but it was unlike the mane of a horse or the hair of man. About its head was a wide crown of horns as obsidian as its talons, each moving outward and inward as it breathed. Its snout was long, rigid, and bony, the nostrils flaring at each inhale. Under its scaled lips the dragon was equipped further with carnivorous teeth, each tooth knocked this way and that by years of wild chases for food that had been devoured into its powerful armored snapping jaw.

"It's bigger looking than I remember now that it isn't just flying away," Longinus whispered. They had all assumed a size of a few more than ten lengths, but now they all agreed it could be no less than twenty.

"Basimick," Cassius continued to whisper. "You're a brave lad. Can we count on you to keep eyes on the beast while we set the shooter?"

Basimick remembered his father's words about following the dragon away but he knew that if it were stopped here then all the danger would be over. He smiled at Cassius, "Can you guarantee the kill?"

"If it stays asleep it will give us the time for a good proper shot."

Basimick nodded and let the two get to work on rebuilding the powerful bow. While they quietly worked he attempted as silently as he could to get to the lip of the rise to closer inspect the dragon. He looked at the creature with wonder and a new hatred that the day before he could have confused with excitement. "Cassius?"

The shout surprised the hunters. "Hushed whispers, lad. Don't want to wake it." Suddenly horror fell upon the group as the dragon became restless.

"We might need to retreat," Longinus tapped Cassius' shoulder.

"I'll distract it," Basimick looked at them as they tried to shy away from the idea. "I offered to help, didn't I?"

Before Cassius could recommend fleeing, Basimick left down the rise into the narrowing chasm. "That is a brave lad."

Longinus got back to work on the weapon. "Come now, for him and the Empire. Waste no time while he risks his skin."

The crevice became shaded as he got nearer to the waking beast and he noticed that the valley began to close from above. Basimick still moved toward it but at every step he would get stricken with nerves and he lumbered forward in sputters. Slowly he got closer and as he did the beast became double the size. Fear began to grip him and the excitement withered entirely. The dragon's great eye opened and it was lit with incredible color like a wildfire hidden behind the sliver of a snake's eye. The very texture of it danced like flames and seemed to capture Basimick in a trance.

Olag of Fire rose ever upward until its height was over twice that of the tallest house in the Kurrum. Its chest was broad and powerful, its legs were the width of large trees, and the air was as wild as a storm when its wings moved outward to stretch. A vicious glow emanated from its intense eyes and the light from within them came out like magical beams. The dragon opened its maw and inside was a forked tongue ensnared in a cage of fangs that were each the length of his arm, shoulder to wrist. The strange hair of its mane shot up straight and a whooshing gust escaped the dragon's throat where at last the tenseness of all its muscles broke so that the creature relaxed from its waking. "I am met by a lone child, disturbed by nothing more than an insect at my bedside? You would dare to approach me while I slumber, boy? What nerve you must have to greet me this way, human."

Basimick was afraid and stayed silent. His hand was shaking but somehow he had managed to reach across himself and grab the pommel of his father's sword.

"I would avoid that, child," the dragon jested. "You have not yet claimed to me your purpose or given me my due respects. Tell me, boy, is it a heart that you yearn for? You men are all motivated as such that my skinned hide could warrant the affection of your chosen. Knights of old with honor more mighty than thou have tried to take my favors, but they are now not but ash, unburied and long forgotten in the wake of my fiery death."

Basimick did not expect the dragon to speak, nor to do so at length. He had only ever heard the tales of old knights slaying dragons with lances and felling them from the sky with mystical arrows. Not once had any of the stories he knew made the monsters of legend seem intelligent enough to talk. Its voice was low and deep so that it resonated within the foundation to shake rock and bone alike. Basimick let go of the pommel but kept his shaking hand at the ready to reveal the blade still.

"Or is it that you seek fame and glory by my defeat? Is this what drives you, young hero," Olag hissed and from its maw dripped hot juices like a starved dog. Its great eyes widened and the fierce orange light was cast over the tiny youth so intensely that there was no shadow about him. "To bear my skull over your throne or to wear my teeth about your neck as to be glorified no better than the hide of a frightened bear! Is this your desire?"

Basimick stood fully frozen, overcome by fear, and the thought to flee never entered into his mind because of the immense terror that clouded him from any judgment at all. He was so absolutely intimidated by the dragon that he could not even remember why he stood where he did, for what purpose had he dared to approach such a thing at all.

Olag's serpentine neck coiled and his head leaned over Basimick so that its nostrils could strike him with blasts of hot damp air. "No," the dragon bellowed from within its mighty chest. "It is *revenge*. I can smell it on you." Its head returned upward to the air and its laugh was like a boulder falling from the ledge of a long mountain, thunder in the distance, and a great drum being brought to breaking all at once. "I have slain many! If you have come to slay me in vengeance forgive me if I know not for who you will die this day. I am weighed little and I care little for the many names I have vanquished, for their souls are petty when offered to all time." A sudden churning and humming resonated from within Olag's stomach as it laughed even more so. "Sages and lore masters of all your meager civilizations to this day write the names of the dead from Ages when I was yet only a wyrmling."

He had been bold in coming down the slope, excited about coming up the mountains with the hunters, he thought he was strong enough to subdue this dragon and prove himself, but now Basimick felt small. He was small. Never before had he been so meek in his heart, yet here he was so inferior to this enemy that he could no longer find his voice and he remained absolutely silent.

"You have disappointed me, tiny human. Not a single word have you uttered, either friendly or not. Of all my conquests in my long years you have said the least, and to not yell or grovel, but to remain so silent. You I will remember as the most pathetic adversary I have yet destroyed. Keep your secrets! Take them all to the grave if that is your wish!" Olag opened its massive maw and the forked tongue lashed about at the dangerous cage of teeth as the orange glow of fire came to life deep within its throat.

Distraction, Basimick remembered at last. He had done a fair job of it without much thinking; he may have been a natural at it perhaps. From a great distance away the siege crossbow whipped the air and the javelin spear whistled with invisible speed. It struck into the dragon's ribs and punctured through its scaly hide. The projectile entered, and then with all the gore it could tear away from the dragon's innards, the javelin ripped from the other side. What power the bow must have had, the weapon still flew and then struck the rock after some distance more. As if it were struck by a crack of lightning, the valley sounded out like thunder and the javelin spear buried its head along with most of its metal shaft into the stone, sending flakes of rock in all directions.

The light of the inner fire faded from Olag's mouth and Basimick was forced to cover his head as the dragon screeched with pain. The echoes of the dragon were louder than the weapon's devastation. "Hunters," it screamed, and the range of the Ash Mountains were filled with noise. "Hunters come to slay the villain!"

The dragon writhed in pain and its serpentine neck flinched to and fro as it recovered from the blow. Basimick, with a trembling hand, drew out his sword and pointed it against the flailing beast. As the mighty claws came to life Basimick stepped away, dodging the talons as the dragon writhed. He stumbled as the wings flared and a gale sent a cloud of dust away in a powerful jet.

"You cannot defeat me like I were a lesser dragon, hunters. I am the Champion of Fire! I am the instrument of Morganna's chaos! I have the flesh of a god and no less than the power of such. My hearts are inextinguishable, my life is unstoppable." Olag took a deep breath and dark black blood gushed from its wound onto the rock where it hissed with immeasurable heat. "I am the fire!"

Another bolt whistled through the air and struck true into the monster. The javelin rang as it bounced from Olag's chest and clattered to the ground. Where it hit was a terrible dent in the dragon, its scales collapsed where a rib must have been smashed.

Olag no longer looked pained. The surprise had passed and anger made the dancing fire in its eyes glow more fiercely. The glow cast crisp shadows around the crevice as it scanned for its enemy. "I will find you, hunter. For now I will be satisfied with your child ward. Watch as this mute is slain because of your failures." Its great talons lifted above Basimick's sword that pointed toward the dragon's palm and followed it over his head so that he stood like a thorn from the ground. A third javelin struck over the back and the twang sounded like a gong as several heavy scales came loose and clattered to the stone. Blood hissed and scorched the rock.

The strength that the dragon had prepared was not lessened by its wounds and Olag plunged upon Basimick with its talons outstretched. Fear was all Basimick had inside him, yet his hands stayed true. As the menacing claws fell at last the tip of the sword lit with a silver spark that cracked like thunder and pushed the dragon's massive arm away. Basimick was frightened that it might have been death passing before his eyes but as he looked up he saw the dragon glaring at him with furious surprise.

"A strange instrument for a child." Olag's eyes narrowed and the glow was a sharp beam upon the hilt of the sword. With a deep breath that released more blood from its wounds, the dragon began to take quick hissing gasps through its nostrils. "If I shall not have you, boy, then I shall destroy your spirit until you have nothing left." Its wings unfurled and Basimick fell back as the gust ripped through the narrow valley. Even with its tremendous weight, the enormous dragon lifted gracefully into the air. Wings outstretched, Olag glided down the side of the barren mountain slope, over the tips of trees, and in moments it passed over the foothills, out of sight, into the west.

Cassius ran, leaning left to right to get his shorter stature moving faster, and he went to Basimick who had yet to get up from the dragon's wind. "Lad! Lad, wake!" He dropped to a knee and smiled, thankful to see the young assistant awake and breathing. "Thank Christianna, you survived. I've not seen anyone get so close to a beast and say the same."

Basimick was lifted to sitting and Cassius held him up. "I think I'm okay. I am shivering. Is that normal?"

"Loose nerves. It will pass soon."

"I don't know what happened, Cassius. Why did Olag leave?"

Hesitantly Cassius tried to take the hilt of Basimick's sword but it seared his hand. "Darn dragon blood," he shouted as he let the weapon go from his hand. Basimick reached out and the shivering lightened as the youth gripped his blade. Cassius smiled as Basimick held tight to the hilt, "I would hold onto that. I'm sorry that my own weapon-"

"No," Basimick stopped the thought. "I saw it. It should have worked." He looked around the walls of the crevice and saw the blood splattered everywhere.

Longinus arrived and brought them both to their feet with a heave. "We wounded it this time for sure. Saw it bleeding all the way down the mountainside. Empowered by an evil god is only worth so much to a few more shots I reckon, if that is the case.``

It might have been the nerves still shaking Basimick's hands but it gave him an eagerness that he had never felt before. "I think I can distract it again."

Cassius shook his head, "Out of the question."

"Wouldn't risk it," Longinus added. "Hoped all you had to do was help watch it sleep. I couldn't forgive myself if it had taken another comrade."

Basimick laughed, his nerves recovering by insincere bravado, "Olag didn't want me. It just wants my spirit." Realization stole the grin from his face. *The dragon was going to Kurrum.*

CHAPTER XIII
RETURNING TO KURRUM

The three had an easier time pulling the cart downhill and made better speed. Basimick pulled in double shifts, telling the other two that he had to return as quickly as he could. The pathways down the Ash Mountains made him uneasy as he could not see over the ridge to where Kurrum waited in the Ash Wood below. They entered into more familiar areas and when Basimick was confident that he could begin sprinting to his village he begged to leave.

The look that the hunters gave him were melancholy, but they urged him onward if he needed to, warning him also that they would not be far behind and would meet him there. Basimick ran down the rest of the mountain, his arms were scraped from careless passage through the underbrush, and he nearly fell from the cliff sides of the lake trying to get up the loose ledges quickly. When he tired he would walk until he had the air to sprint again. He could no longer remember the fear he had felt from the dragon for the desperation he had in his heart kept him moving toward home.

The Ash Wood had a heavy haze in it. Smoke was clinging to the leaves so that even when Basimick finally arrived at the familiar creek side where his father had fought the bear it seemed foreign. He made a tired step into the shallow and fell into the water but the cold shook him awake. He rushed against the creek and came to a charred scorch in the woods. Panic set in and he knew the dragon had beaten him back to his home.

The trees were barren of leaves, their trunks were black from fire, and the view that had once been blocked by the canopy was torn open. He could see through the woods into Kurrum where the thickest plumes of smoke billowed forth and filled the forest. He could see other lodges amidst the trees and the dragon seemed absolute in its destruction. He passed the bridge but did not dare call out or dare to look at Bassar's home. He knew if his father were alive he would be helping in the village, and his heart chose to look for his family there.

Basimick moved slowly into the quiet village through where the western gate had stood. There were shells of houses with exhausted wood piles scorched on the ground. There were husks curled together and he began to understand that he was alone. Basimick walked mournfully through it, like a survivor of a long war in a wide graveyard.

They were not far behind, though the hunters were worried that they had allowed too much time for the young village guard to wander alone in the destruction. Cassius rounded what was left of the old western gate. It had burned so that only a corner of charred wood stood to guard what remained. Inside of the devastated wall was ash and before him was a scorched black path of ruin that covered the entire length of Crossroad. Basimick was plain to see as they slowly marched down Mainroad. He was moving about to help if he could, yet Cassius knew by experience that there would not be another soul to find. The dragon hunters moved the cart toward the last bit of recognizable structure, the first floor of the bishop's stone building, where only a few scorched rocky pillars now stood.

"Lad," Cassius was quiet but he seemed to shout across the silent place. "Come and share your grim news with me."

"Do not be afraid to speak," Longinus added.

Basimick lifted a plank of wood and the smoke struck his eyes. As he waved about to relieve the sting from the smoking board he saw the charred remains and set the wood down gently to cover it back up. "Marccus, I am so sorry." He looked in a wide circle and for a moment he could not tell if he was dizzy or if the world was spinning about him. "I don't know why I chose to do that," he shouted. "My father told me not to do that. We shouldn't have tried to kill it here!"

Cassius and Longinus were silent as the young guard continued to scream at the burning wreckage. At last Basimick closed his eyes and moved toward the hunters who sat against a secure length of the stone wall. Cassius made a hollow smile but even he could not hide the deep remorse. His eyes were red with tears as the hunter looked around, blaming himself also for the destruction. "First steps are always the hardest."

"I remember when I was a young lad," Longinus said, eyeing the smoldering ruins of the dwarven doorway at the east end of Mainroad. "A young wyrm came from the west and moved into a mountain pass just north of my village. Everyone was so afraid and many had chosen to leave that very day. My family chose not to go. We thought it would go further than it did."

Cassius tried to hold himself together and hugged Basimick who was beginning to sob as Longinus continued.

"It was the next day, and I remember those woods were burning. I could smell the dragon fire, and I can recall it even when I am far from it, for it was unlike anything natural. My father, a good hunter, shot at it, and of a dozen arrows only one struck true, but it meant little to a beast like that." Longinus wiped his face with his sleeve as he began to cry as well. "The dragon spoke to him, told him that death was too merciful, and he forced my father to witness everything burn. I had a mother, and a sister, and everyone from Pinewatch, but all I have now are memories."

Basimick was sobbing deeper so Cassius asked, "What came next, Longinus?"

"I was away, but my father sought to kill the dragon. He was mad, must have been driven there by all the loss. He was only armed with his hunting bow, he could do little against it, and the dragon had already played enough, so it took him too."

Longinus opened his arms and Basimick shifted away from one embrace to another when Cassius began to speak. "I had a lovely wife, I did. I had two children, and one due any day. It was Sepa, we were celebrating Harvesti time in the city. I had been a salesman back then, made a lot of good sovereigns trading to the dwarves. I was in the right spot for trade, just between the dwarven Iron Gate and their ports of Malenclutch north a ways. They were always happy to see me when I came, for I knew the tongue and brought them the news."

He took a deep breath to fight the memory from being too overwhelming and then he continued, "I had a hand in building up Iron Gate back then, using my skill to ferry the siege equipment from the port to there in my good carriages." He kicked the cart resting near them and laughed before he began to tear up with everyone else. "I was coming back from Malenclutch when I saw my city burning. Walls were holding in the fire like an oven and the smoke was black. It smelled like more than just the wood burning. I saw it, like a vile bat, like a beast from the Hells of Annabel herself."

He paused and looked through the smoke into the sky. "I had hoped of course, even while everything seemed doomed, so I took the siege weapon I was toting, armed it, aimed it by my own self, and fired. I must have been blessed for all the bad luck in the world because that lance struck true."

Basimick looked up from Longinus' chest and gazed at them both. "Why do they do these things?"

Cassius was no longer smiling, but he was not distant. He was closer now than Basimick had ever felt to anyone. "If we could ask them, maybe we could have been dragon diplomats instead."

"We almost had it, didn't we? We almost killed Olag."

"A blow like that would have slain any lesser wyrm," Longinus shook Basimick proudly.

"Why didn't it?"

Cassius had a look of disappointment. "Olag of Fire is a great force from very ancient days. It may just be that in place of a heart there is the boon of Morganna herself. I have heard that a dwarf stricken with the gifts of the Earth Mother Helena could sunder a castle in a single swing of a hammer. I worry about what Olag is capable of if such a rumor were true."

"Would that wound have hurt it any?"

"Immensely," Longinus assumed.

"Where would it go if it were hurt? Olag isn't from here, right?"

"No it isn't," Cassius grew excited again and got to his feet. "It came from the west, out of the molten lands of Montontra."

"I have heard of that place," Basimick said nervously as Longinus began to get up on his own feet.

"Orc lands," the tall one said. "A volcanic valley where evil things live nearest to Morganna. Everything you've heard does not compare to the truth of that place."

"Olag would go there?"

"A dragon of this magnitude is well known," Cassius said confidently. "It keeps a lair in the mouth of the greatest volcano, closest to its master, in the cauldron of Mhat-Ozogra."

Basimick looked around briefly but could not gaze at Kurrum for long. "If we go, can we finish it?"

Cassius quickly shot a smile at Longinus before the emotions overtook them again, "That sounds like duty for a dragon hunter."

Basimick couldn't smile. *Of course I am not a dragon hunter,* he thought. *Too young, too immature,* and all the excuses his sister could give swelled in his mind.

Longinus laughed as best he could given the circumstances, "Welcome to our party, master Basimick."

Cassius pulled out a metal coin, much like his own, and held it out for Basimick. "For striking the foe, not for being the bait."

Basimick reached out and took it with a firm handshake that pulled him onto his own feet, "but I-"

"You may have done more than even the javelin. Don't sell yourself short. Might be near two centuries now since anyones used a sword against a dragon. You have more courage than most, lad."

Longinus patted Basimick on the shoulder and offered a seat on the cart, "Welcome, brother. Let's not linger here long though. We don't want bad memories gathering or ghosts treading on us."

"Closest rest is Ovelclutch. It's a few days, but we can make it by the roads from here," Cassius fixed the yolk on his shoulders and picked up the cart for the first turn. "Want to lead us the way out of the woods, lad?"

Basimick nodded and thought to look around one last time but chose to avoid the heartache. "Just out the gate and," his words trailed off into silence.

"What is it, lad?"

"Just that there isn't a gate anymore." Basimick took a deep breath as Longinus held him in the back of the cart. He tried to speak but it was raspy and tired, "The way west will take us through Ash Wood."

Longinus nodded and spoke up for Basimick, "West road, Cassius."

"Aye, lads. Rest now. Turns are coming for the cart, surely."

CHAPTER XIV
THE SHOW

The Red Circus had traveled from beyond the East Border Spine and came south along the Marching Road to the Midland capital city of Armontrosia. It was a massive city with towers of incredible height piercing along the horizon and as days passed in their travels they could see the lights in the thousands matching the stars of the night sky. They journeyed around the walls and Ulric managed his way through the front gates with a fair amount of charisma to pass the guards. As the circus entered the city Ulric's assistant Lin met with several officials so that the troupe could make camp in one of the many city forums. It wasn't long before a crowd gathered for the usual raising of the tent and the juggler Haurus began to entice new patrons to their show.

When everything was set Haurus was at the front entry to the great pavilion of the Red Circus. He more often than not performed at the entry during times they were in the city, for the crowds were so immense that they would have to wait to see the main shows.

Kalara came from around the tent and kicked the showman stump he was perched on, "All alone, Haurus?"

"My partner is preparing for her show is all," he smiled at the patrons and began to pull knives from hidden places among his red leather outfit. "Come to manage the crowd with me, rope walker?"

"I am more of a premier show. Big tent only. That's why I've already been asked by Ulric to join the meeting tonight," she waved her hand to present herself with a wild vanity.

"A meeting tonight?"

"Maybe it's just for the real shows, Haurus."

"Ah, but without her or I there would be none drawn to the tent to see your act," he laughed in jest but Kalara had already left and he found that he was already engrossed in an act without much thought for the distraction. He had six knives juggling in the air at this point of his show and he was still able to take the sovereigns from customers wanting in. Several of the people felt they had to duck as he leaned over from his stump, but he promised the onlookers that they were never in any real danger. The sharp blades continued to dance through the air, flashing as they caught the sun's light and it forced some to cower away from the sudden bursts of the metal's glare.

The juggler danced around the next group, invited them into the tent to separate those that would have to wait for the next performance, and then he led the way inside. He leaned close to the crowd and asked an older nobleman who was caught by Haurus' charm and wanderlust, "Would you like more?" The throng followed Haurus and they all meandered through the opening into the dark of the immense pavilion, but the old man did not seem to care about the other wonders as he nodded to answer the juggler with childish delight. Haurus bent forward to grab at his boots, allowing the knives to dip down near his knees, and then they danced around his back to be tossed upwards at twice the height.

Suddenly, as though by magic, there were a dozen knives whirling through the air. Haurus brought them into a routine of catch and toss, the sharp dangerous blades not once biting their master's hands.

Haurus had captured the attention of many more well-dressed visitors and he continued to elevate his performance as he pointed them to their seats around the edge of the sand pit which only a few patrons managed to notice had been dug into the hard stone of the forum plaza. He began to spin in circles but not one of the dozen knives fell. "More," cried the old man hoping that the juggler's show could offer such a request and Haurus was eager to enhance the display.

As the knives fell from their loop in the air Haurus began to count. "One," he shouted and the knife flew out of his grasp, striking a small bale of hay that had suddenly appeared in the dark behind him. The old man applauded at the perfect bullseye. "Two, three." The blades found new marks, dead center, to the low left and high right, into bales dangled around the scene out of view until just that moment. On his command yet another four blades twirled out, this time each one evenly fanning out through the crowd and each one struck into the hearts of no less than four scarecrows, each one dressed as assassins hidden among the seats. Surprise caught the patrons sitting beside the scarecrows but the old man's laughter at their shock made them smile as though Haurus had just rescued them from a deadly attack.

Five knives were looping through the air as Haurus continued to leap and dance, the blades finding his hands only to return into the air with quick skill. "Eight, nine, ten," he shouted again and the old man laughed with his whole belly at the excitement. The knives struck true into the chests of several jesters creeping through the dark sand pit, their masks making them appear as wild caricatures of their noble viewers.

Haurus then juggled with only two knives, yet the nobles were still excited to see what could be done with them as he managed the pair of blades in a single hand. "I am glad to have held your attention," Haurus said to everyone as the last few took their seats, but especially to the old man who still waited to see more. "Prepare yourselves now for more than what this humble juggler's simple act can bring and be amazed by only the beginning of our wild tour from around the strange lands of Nhearn. She comes from a land harsh and terrifying, but she was plucked from the dying deserts, tempted away by a traveling lover, and now she has come with us to show you the power of movement and the dangers of delight. I present to you the dazzling dancing damsel herself!" He threw one of the knives and it moved as straight as an arrow to the very top of the tent where it struck a glass lantern that dangled above the center ring. As it shattered a ball of fire erupted. The entire tent was hit by heat and lit by a sparkling fire that rained down like a curtain over the stage.

All at once the room grew dark as the fire feigned and withered on the sand inside the center ring. The nobles who had gathered inside strained to see anything within the tent as their eyes needed to adjust to the lighting once again. As their sight returned Haurus was ready. "Twelve," he whispered to himself, as though it needed to be said to avoid bad luck and ensure that his final throw would stay as true as he had practiced. He flung the knife as accurately as a dwarven crossbow and as straight as the bolt. The blade vanished into the dark of the vast pavilion and all Haurus could see was the single candle lit in the middle of the tent. *Hit the target,* he prayed for success.

Sparks flew from the center ring like many bolts of lightning, flashing, casting strange shadows over the faces of the nobles. Everyone's eyes adjusted and then set on a glowing ball of fire as though it were the last grip before the edge of darkness. It rose up and the flames took deep breaths from the ornate orifices adorning the ball. It went higher and higher until it violently dropped like a man at the gallows. The crowd gasped as though harm had come to the little ball of fire.

Left then right, slowly, as though the effort were tiring, the ball swung like a holy Christiannan church censer until it was then fully lit and wreathed in bright flame. Jesters lit the lanterns again and the tent was cast in dim light so that they might see her, the dancer in the center ring. From her hand dangled a fine chain strung to the top of the fireball that moved as a pendulum without her stirring in the slightest.

Silence was heavy in the tent and the roar of fire in the small chained ball was felt in the hearts of the crowd. Left then right, the fire ball swung back and forth, rising ever upward in a ring around the dancer, and as it reached its full height above her head it rang like a bell. The gentle ball that captured the love of the crowd erupted with anger and white sparks shot out again in great flashes like lightning.

"Lucky thirteen," and Haurus bowed to the old man beside him who was thoroughly impressed with the juggler and he disappeared into the depths of the tent, his act finally ended.

The fervor of her dance was gripping and the ball of fire was swinging all about her madly. The thin chain weaved itself about her arms and legs to bind her as the flames drew near, yet a leap or a twist would send the danger away again. In and out, through and over, side to side, the ball did not cease its violent orbit and she did not dare end the captivating dance. It was dazzling, just as promised, and she completed the final spins that drew out the last of the fire's fuel. As the fire began to pass away the orbiting ball came to a gentle rest in the sand.

Up on their feet, the nobles all clapped and roared for her. The old man who knew that the knife thrower had a role to play began to whistle and call for him to take a bow as well.

The dazzling dancing damsel took the bow alone in the center ring, but no one seemed bothered by Haurus' absence and they continued cheering all the same. She gently gathered the chain and the crowd still clapped a while before hushing themselves as a jester came out with a small wooden box. She cradled the hot thing, gently put it away, and then quickly waved her hands to ward off the heat while the crowd laughed for the humor of it all. One more bow and the girl was lifted up by a sudden surge of jesters to be taken away from the center ring.

CHAPTER XV
THE RITUAL

Haurus stood amidst the crates and carriages as a crowded circle entered into the great red tent. He was sure that Mebruk and most of the older members of the circus had run off for a night in the city with the allowance that Ulric had given them and wasn't sure why a group had come back to the tent.

"Finally got the invitation, Haurus?"

"Lin," Haurus jumped. "No, I don't think I really did. Kalara said something about the meeting."

"Are you sure that you want to," Lin smiled. "You are a good friend, Haurus. I love you, but Ulric would be rather upset if he didn't invite you properly."

"I've been in the circus for a while now. How did Kalara get invited before me?"

Lin shrugged but his face gave away the secret.

"I know Ulric isn't very fond of me."

"But he does enjoy how much money you bring to the circus." Lin sighed. "Do you want to come? I am part of the inner circle with master Reddon. I could take the lashings for inviting someone myself."

"If it isn't too much trouble," Haurus smiled. He reached out and hugged Lin, "And if it is I'll give you my allowance for it."

"That's a good deal, that is. Come then."

Haurus walked inside with Lin through the main entry that had its laces undone as though the Red Circus was still open for showings. The pair of them looked around the gathering and could see the new members, most of which were young runaways or orphans who worked managing the crowd for lack of show skills. There were others around, like Kalara who had several of her shows during the early morning entertaining as a rope walker, or Tarmont who could breathe fire like the dragons. None of them were very old, though the newer additions seemed far younger than those who had been traveling with the Red Circus.

"Some of these people were put to work today," Haurus jabbed Lin half-jokingly. "How was I unaware of this?"

"If I told you I would be betraying Ulric," Lin tried to hide from his friend's hands and pulled away. "I don't do a whole lot around here, but I am good at being master Reddon's assistant. I'd like to keep it that way so I can still travel with the great juggler."

Haurus made a wide smile, "You have done very well."

"I have a few more responsibilities to get to before it begins. I didn't want to say anything about it, but I think Hilde is here too."

"She told me she had business with Ulric," Haurus nodded, realizing that she had told the truth but kept the secret better than Kalara. He said a quick farewell to Lin and moved through the groupings of jesters and coin servants hoping to find her.

He spotted her quickly, his eyes drawn to her, a power he had developed in their travels together. She sat alone near the sand pit at the middle of the tent atop a crate waiting for the meeting to begin. He crept along, moving unnoticed through them, something he was alarmingly skillful at, and he quickly found himself beside her. She still had paint on her face and her hair was as wild as it had been during her last show. "What are you doing here," he asked in a whispered tone.

Everyone present was speaking loudly as though nothing in the tent could be heard by any passerby wandering outside, and Hilde had to lean against Haurus to hear him, "What's that now?"

"I wasn't expecting to find you here."

"I wasn't expecting you either, sweetheart," she smiled at him. "And the show today, you said I left home to follow *you*?"

"I will forgive you for keeping secrets if you let me get away with lying to the nobles."

She seemed offended. "Secrets? I am the leading act," she said confidently with only a slight air of jesting. "Is it not expected that I would be here?" She looked up at Haurus from her seat and saw that he was still dressed in his leather show jerkin while everyone around had brought their simple white clothes that were worn when the circus was closed. He looked out of place but he had also removed the red paint from his face and it made him stand apart from the others more so. She was suddenly frowning, her eyes giving away a sad thought, "Planning to leave?"

Haurus, to her relief, shook his head, "And leave you here? My mood would be far worse anywhere else."

"Sorry I didn't tell you," she smiled once more. "Come here then, juggler." She pulled him down by the collar and pushed her cheek across his so that some of her red face paint rubbed off on him. "There, now you look the part." Haurus could not speak back as the warmth of her cheek refused to be forgotten. She smiled wider and the dimples on her face seemed to only further remove him from the noise of the pavilion. There was no longer sound, or torch light, or anything, or anyone, except him and her. "If you weren't expecting me then Ulric did not ask you to be here, did he Haurus?"

"Lin," he pointed slowly but could not find their friend in the crowd and he felt a bit silly for it. "I came with him after I caught Kalara saying there was a meeting of some kind."

"It's for the new members of the circus, I heard."

Haurus tried to snap out of his trance over Hilde, but he could not break away entirely and he spoke slowly, "I am not new?"

"We've missed the last few though, Haurus."

Haurus nodded, still trying to get his wits to come back. "What about you? You aren't new."

"This is my first time coming also. Ulric likes to host these anytime there are enough people to make it proper. I was invited, but Lin was the one who convinced me to come. He told me Ulric makes him come to each meeting but he always has to leave early, so he asked me to see what was happening."

"Lin didn't ask me about any of that."

"You weren't really invited," she laughed.

Suddenly the tent was silent. The crowd turned about together as Ulric arrived at the entrance of the tent behind them and he dragged a cart with several crates laid upon it. "Welcome all," he said with a ceremonious bow. "Lin, your assistance please." Lin was suddenly at the doorway from his hiding place in the crowd and he pulled the cart the rest of the way into the pit of the center ring.

Ulric Reddon pulled a wooden crate off the cart and set it in the sand as close to the middle of the pavilion as he could manage. He gazed upward to ensure that the tallest point of the tent was directly above the crate. It had a lock on each side and two on its front to seal the crate fully. Other than those iron locks the crate had no markings or decorations; it was as simple as could be made. "For those of you with second thoughts I would ask that you take your leave now. I know that we here at the Red Circus are not the most upstanding citizens, many the opposite, but I refuse to lead the blind. When I open this box you will not leave here without her blessing to do so. You will all need to be polite and you must never interrupt her. I will be honest with you, my duty is to bring in new members for her and teach them of her ways. I hope that some of you are willing, but I have not lived as long as I have with any moment spent on regret."

"No regrets, Haurus," Hilde whispered.

"I love you," He replied and she grabbed his hand tightly.

Ulric continued on, "I would not want your choice here to weigh on my mind. Leave now if you would avoid this fate, or stay and gain the blessings of my Lady."

A quiet moment passed but not one of Ulric's guests left the tent. Ulric then nodded and the entrance to the tent was sealed shut from the outside as Lin departed from the ceremony.

"Let us begin then," and with a showman's flare, Ulric spun the crate so that the side with two locks faced toward him. He drew out a metal ring from within his royal cloak that contained no less than one hundred keys, each one unique in tong, color, and age. He pulled a specific key and stepped aside to unlock one of the side irons. Ulric then moved in such a way as to respect the crate, going to the opposite side where he pulled a different key from the ring to remove the next lock. He kneeled at the front of the crate and took two unique keys for the next two locks. No one seemed to recall what key went where and before anyone could offer a guess the keys were hidden away in the depths of his cloak once more.

He then slowly, reverently, laid the crate down into the sand to be opened. He held it by either side and gently it came apart so that it was split perfectly in two halves. The crowd gathered near and they could see that one side had a silver mirror made to fit into the bottom of the crate as though it were just a regular mirror set into a deep frame. Fit into the bottom of the other half of the crate was a mirror so dark it could only be described as black.

"One at a time. Come Tarmont." The great beast of a man kneeled before the front of the crate so that both mirrors were set to either side before him. "Look into the silver mirror," Ulric said and Tarmont leaned over the mirror where he saw his portrait plainly. "What is it you wish to change?"

"I wish I was real," Tarmont said into the mirror. "I wish I could breathe the true flame."

"Keep your wants," Ulric touched Tarmont's shoulder and then pointed at the other side of the crate. "Look now into the black mirror and wish, my friend."

Tarmont leaned over and could see his reflection in the black gloss. "I wish to breathe fire," he said aloud after a long pause.

Ulric told Tarmont, "Do not look away, and you may feel nothing, but do not be fooled. You have been given what you have asked for, friend." Ulric then held his finger to his lips and hushed the already quiet man. "Do not be afraid of who you are. Do you understand?"

Tarmont nodded.

"Be polite, yes?"

Tarmont nodded again.

"Look back at the silver mirror."

Tarmont leaned back over to the silver mirror and the crowd around him tried to watch the movements of his face. He began to scowl, then he squinted his eyes before looking fearful, and then disgusted. As he let a breath out from his nose a light shone about his face and the mustache he was proud of became singed by fire. He shouted with pain and from his mouth came an eruption, a torrent of fire not unlike what he had done at his own show. He shouted with terror until at last he could shout no longer and Tarmont tried then to take a breath in. Some tried to call out to him, but everyone knew the dangers of breathing fire. Tarmont had taken it to his lungs, and he fell into the sand, dead.

Everyone was silent until Kalara stepped forward and spoke up for the crowd, "Tarmont was breathing fire, he got his wish. Why did he-"

Ulric raised his hand and hushed her. "The rules," he whispered. "Listen and be silent. This is no djinn or ghast. There is no irony or twist of cruel magic." He raised his voice as though he were frustrated, "Tarmont died because he upset my Lady." He regained himself. "Be polite, do not interrupt, and do not be ungrateful." He pointed to Kalara and she stepped forward with terrible hesitancy. "Come and look in the silver mirror." They both leaned over the crate. Ulric asked, "What is it you wish to change?"

Kalara suddenly lost her hesitancy, "I wish to be unafraid. I would wish that there was no height great or small that may bring harm to me."

"Keep your wants. Look now into the black mirror and wish, my friend."

Kalara leaned over and could see her reflection in the black gloss. "I wish no fall could harm me," she said aloud so that the crowd could hear her.

Ulric nodded and Kalara remembered his words. She leaned back to the silver mirror and smiled. She bowed to the crate and stood up to retreat back into the crowd behind her.

"Did it work," someone asked.

Kalara looked at Ulric and shook her head. "I was asked not to try anything until after the ritual had ended. She had said to me, *what good is faith if she must prove it to us.*"

Ulric pointed to the next, "Come now."

The ritual continued, the same words, leaning to silver, then black, then back to silver once more. Most managed to return to the crowd, but some were unable to hide their disgust. One had wished to breathe underwater and had suffered so that they could not breathe in the open air. Another had simply wanted perfect hair always and was brought to such terror that they began to cut it all off with sheers they discovered somewhere within the pavilion. They continued well beyond ridding themselves of their hair, cutting into the scalp and then to the bone until they passed away in frantic shouts to the bitter end.

At long last young Hilde was pointed at and as she kneeled before the mirrors Ulric let out a heavy sigh. "Part of me wishes that you had chosen not to come to this ritual," he whispered. "I worry for you as a daughter."

"I know, but that is why I had to come. I want to be part of your clan." Hilde had heard many wishes now and it was plain on her face that she was truly excited for her turn.

"Look into the silver mirror," he said again. "What is it you wish to change?"

Hilde smiled at her reflection, the red face paint a bit smeared, but still well enough intact to see the decoration that it was meant to be. "I don't want to die, ever. I want to be young forever." The crowd smiled, impressed at the grand wish she had made, all but one who had only wished to make flowers bloom and was now sour with disappointment.

"Keep your wants. Look now into the black mirror and wish, my friend."

Hilde leaned over to the black glossy mirror and met her eyes in the reflection but in an instant they were not her eyes. She could no longer see her own face; it was like she could no longer remember what she looked like, as though she were a stranger to herself. *Keep my wants,* she remembered.

A beautiful soothing voice, indescribable and unimaginable, came to her. *"I see you,"* it whispered from beyond the mirror, but the voice also came from within her skull. *"How pretty you are, girl. I sense cleverness in you. What is your desire? What is the price for your servitude?"*

Hilde found it difficult to stay focused or feel grounded and her desires were but fleeting thoughts. *Keep my wants*; she struggled against her own racing mind to remember.

"Jealousy I sense in you. You desire magic, money, and all the talents of your associates."

Hilde fought the myriad of daydream fantasies of other people's riches and their abilities. They were her own feelings that were rising up, but she knew that these were brief moments of wonder, times she had thought *if I could do that*. She knew that everything being shown to her now were thoughts of passing, as they had been in those real moments.

"I sense great want. Beauty, perhaps?"

Hilde felt compelled to ask for it, lasting beauty, but quickly that faded with self-acknowledgement. *Keep my wants,* her mind repeated.

"There is power with you," it said. *"You are not so simple like the others. They were very easy to purchase. I know what you seek and I would deliver it should you ask me kindly."*

"I wish to live forever," she seemed to scream at the reflection, the effort to speak was like lifting a heavy weight from her chest.

"A long while, forever is. A place I myself have yet to see. My servant, take my blessing that you may do my bidding."

Hilde heard Ulric repeat, "Look into the silver mirror," but his voice was mirrored by the indescribable voice from the black reflection. Hilde leaned over and she could see herself in the mirror, her own face still wearing the red paint and her hair was recognizably wild, but it was not her that she saw. It were as though a person dressed in an outfit like her and then learned to move like she did so that they could hide through a strange window in front of her as she watched. She locked eyes with the reflection and could see something deep in the dark of her eyes as though a creature were lurking in a long black tunnel.

"Are you frightened? Do you find yourself revolting?"

"Thank you," Hilde smiled. "With honor and love, I serve."

"Precious thing."

Hilde got up from her knees and saw that Ulric was filled with relief that she came out on the other side of the ritual unscathed. She moved back into the crowd and everyone let out a deep sigh of relief for Hilde.

Ulric frowned and then pointed to the next candidate. "Haurus, be wise," he reminded the child, but it was said with the disapproving expectation that this one would not survive. "Come."

Haurus was hesitant but Hilde's smile drove him to the center ring before the two mirrors in the crate. He was directed to kneel and he looked into the silver mirror as instructed. Ulric gave the repetitive script to him and then asked that he lean toward the black mirror. He managed to avoid saying anything aloud and the crowd was just as silent as they tried to hear him, everyone waiting for the young reckless Haurus to burst or wail.

"I sense strong conviction within you. More so than any other." His eyes met a distant thing in his own dark reflection. He could hear its voice in his head and he could hear it from beyond the mirror. *"I asked every other what they desire most, but I imagine your servitude would be-"*

"Hilde," he answered. "I wish to be with her for as long as she'd choose to have me."

Ulric seemed more insulted than he did stern, "You are interrupting, Haurus."

The distant reflection of the thing suddenly came upon the glass and its face overtook his own. It was a monster, a demonic creature from the Hells of Annabel, but around it was a shroud of black smoke that hid the terrible aspects away and draped around its form were visions of beauty that comforted the horrible apparitions. "I like this one, Ulric," it said through the reflecting box. "I can use this one. He is bold." Hilde stepped forward from the crowd and held her hand out as though she needed to catch him from a terrible fall. "I can use them both." The thing slid back into the black mirror's depths so that his reflection came back. *"Your wish is granted."*

Ulric was surprisingly pleased that Haurus wasn't destroyed, but he kept a face that was grim for the etiquette of the ritual had been tarnished by the youth's disrespect. "Look at the silver mirror."

Haurus leaned back over to the silver mirror. He saw his face, and the tent, and Ulric who was across from him, but he did not see anything strange. He tried then looking at his eyes and then he found an oddness. *These are not my eyes.* He looked and saw a deep tunnel from the dark of his eyes. He peered within and waiting for him near the deepest reaches of sight was her.

Hilde touched his shoulder and he jumped with a fright, though he should have noticed her coming in the reflection. "What have you done, Haurus?"

"I made a wish."

"It is all wrong," she said solemnly.

Ulric stood up and grabbed him by the scruff of his red leather outfit. "Let me see you," he was pulled to his feet. "Something foul has happened. You are not like the rest of us."

Haurus looked at everyone and they stared back without an answer.

"Look at the black mirror, Haurus," Ulric said with a demanding voice.

He turned away from the ritual to look at Hilde but she turned him around herself, gripping him by the shoulders to face into the black mirror, and he peered as deeply as he could into it. Nothing answered from the darkness and he leaned closer into the mirror as they both commanded. His eyes were still different than they had been before and he looked into them with wonder. As Haurus focused into the depths of his eye he could see her still, sleeping perhaps, holding tight to a shining orb that became the glare of the torchlight as the pavilion returned to the reflection.

"It's me," She said. Haurus looked into Hilde's eyes through the black mirror. "I own your soul?" Hilde picked him up from the ground, grabbed him tightly, and spun him around to face her. "How did you do this?"

"I wished for it," He said confidently. He thought for a moment and stared at her, "What is it that you saw in the mirror?"

Ulric grabbed Haurus by the shoulder and spun him around so that his legs were wrapped around themselves and he relied on them both for balance. "Whose service did you sell yourself to?"

"I wished to be with Hilde."

"Me, Haurus?" Hilde looked ashamed. "But what does that mean for me? Am I still part of all this?"

Ulric let go and Haurus fell into the sand. "Nothing has unraveled. I suspect your blessing is still tied to my Lady in some manner as the rest of us."

Hilde tried to lift Haurus up but he had been spun about so much he had become dizzy. "She wouldn't just give him to me, surrender his soul to me, I mean. I would not think such a gift could be offered."

Haurus at last got to his feet, "Is it all a trick then?"

"Haurus," Ulric frowned, and the tent fell silent at his commanding voice. "All of you, the ritual has ended. Be gone to the night and sleep well."

Kalara shook her head, "What about the ones that didn't make it?"

Ulric Reddon, who often held a respectful and jubilant tone, was no longer radiating such energy. "Don't become a fool now that you are given wishes like in a child's storybook. This is the Red Circus, and it takes care of us."

The crowd looked at the pavilion and became aware of how strange it truly was. Where had the sandpit come from, for none of them had brought sands or had to dig through stone? Where had the seats and props been delivered, for no one needed to bring them? The color of it became haunting as the more bloodied of the fallen initiates seemed to match the pavilion's aesthetic. Quietly they turned to leave through the flap that had now become undone despite Lin's absence.

Ulric then pointed at the pair, "Tell me, what do you know of faith, gods, religion." He closed the mirrors and locked the crate's irons in a specific sequence with specific keys as they shook their heads without answer. "I fear for you. A Goddess is not so easily fooled, and you may have just received a very powerful ally or a tireless and lasting enemy. Come, follow me."

He heaved the crate onto the cart and hid it among the other crates that had come into the pavilion with it.

Haurus attempted to help but Ulric denied it, "It is my duty to care for the mirrors and few may ever do so."

They left the pavilion and followed their leader to his personal carriage which rested near to the back of the caravan ring. As the crate was set away and the area was quiet around them, Ulric asked, "Have you ever heard of Beatrix?"

They shook their heads.

"There are few who know the powers of this God, but among her followers are great nobles, powerful seers, and those who know that she can offer limitlessness if they ask it of her. You are now among those people," he said to Hilde. "Some frown upon her worship however."

"Why," Haurus asked.

"She is dangerous as well," Ulric pointed at the pavilion where the bodies of the ritual may still be residing.

Hilde became worried. "Dangerous? Then why join her? Why worship such a thing?"

Ulric was not offended by her question, but he looked distraught and did not wish to upset her more. "Did you know that Aurora is considered a savior to the people of the Empire-"

"That's the moon goddess," Haurus questioned.

"The full moon, yes," Ulric answered. "But she is the reason for so many more deaths than Beatrix. Aurora purges what she considers vile by purifying it with fire and blade. She is dangerous, yet she is considered utmost to be holy in her ways."

Haurus and Hilde looked around them and the towers of the Imperial city seemed to be watching them now as they realized the citizens could be charged to slay what they deemed wicked.

"Beatrix, to some, may be evil, but is this not just a vanity imposed by those who would claim their own ways as goodness."

"Perhaps," Hilde quietly answered.

Ulric smiled at her, "We may speak more of Beatrix when we leave the city and find more time to ourselves. For now, be among your family."

"What about me?"

"You are among family, Haurus. Your circumstances are strange, but that you are not dead means your soul is not yet given to the Tower of Death. Perhaps it is that Hilde holds your soul and you are bound to her." Ulric stroked his chin with thought. "Give me time to think of what this means, but so long as she is bound to the servitude of Beatrix you should consider yourself a servant of her will also. Your wish has been granted to you after all."

CHAPTER XVI
THE ASSASSINS RETURN

Even with their trained elven eyes they could not see into the spans toward the horizon through the heavy storm clouds. "Any respite," Terica asked as she scanned opposite her companion for any cover from the weather.

"None," Lilium answered with defeat. "Perhaps there are many more days of this rain though."

"Better than all daylight," Terica tried to say enthusiastically. "We could have been exposed out here."

The Grasslands were bare except the grass that stood tall and even in all directions. For any outsider to the lands it could have been a maddening excursion to traverse without any paths or landmarks to guide them. Lilium held her head up and felt the rain on her face. "No shade," she smiled briefly. "Luck is on our side then."

They continued westward through the territory of the nomadic plain elves for only a short while before Terica felt the dread pull back into the pair once more and Lilium could feel the eyes of her companion upon her. "We've no time to rest now," Lilium stated. "Krethnarok is just a bit north when we round the mountains out of the nomad's land."

"I can keep moving."

"You've been silent for most of the way, Terica. For a trained assassin you talk much, but not any longer."

"You have not felt friendly."

"Is it the blade?" Lilium had the dark and vile dagger wrapped in a heavy cloth but it was still strapped to her hip over her own Blackroot blade.

It was such a wicked thing that they could feel its presence, enough so that when they did choose to rest it kept them awake with new anxiety and dread, but Terica knew her companion well enough to see the difference it had been making in the older Blackroot. "You are afraid of it."

"Vanessa needed me to have this blade."

"Has she shown you a target?"

"She conveyed only the knowledge to discover the means of pruning them," Lilium touched the hilt briefly but quickly retreated. "What of your visions? Has she told you anything yet?"

"I am not sure," Terica didn't press any further about the vile weapon. "I had a dream, I think. Just a dream. A memory maybe. It was of my first target, the preacher who was killing stag for some bit of spite on Vanessa. I had to sneak into a human settlement and when I arrived my nerves were thin, but I do not remember hesitating when the time came. I actually did it. I pruned the preacher and became a Blackroot that day."

"You do not fool me, sister Blackroot."

"No, I committed to the command of the Fey Mother, but in the dream I was stopped by something that had not been there before."

"What was this detail," Lilium's jesting attitude became serious.

"It was a fear of something and then I awoke to a bright light."

Lilium noticed that she had become forceful toward her companion and tried to loosen her demeanor. "It could have just been waking perhaps."

When they had begun their trek again Terica waited to ask, "How are the Blackroot chosen?"

Lilium thought a moment, for her induction had been centuries away into the past and her ceremonies made memories fade easily. "I believe Vanessa calls to us, as the thorns of a rose are formed or the razors of grass are honed. It is destiny."

Terica was worried that her questions were revealing disloyalty and she made sure to tell her companion, "I have never denied the callings."

"Death is a burden," Lilium said solemnly. "Our duty is of great importance, but killing is a stain upon the soul."

"The others seem to enjoy it."

"I did not ask the others to join me." Lilium eased her pace beside her companion. "The ending of your dream, tell me again, what was it?"

"I was restrained from acting. It was like a haunt in my memory. My knife was as deadly as it was that day but it was like the strike did not make a cut, more like it had torn through the target, and a light poured out from the wound. I was blinded by it and I awoke." Terica waited to hear what could be interpreted of the vision and a long silence lingered between them.

"You still have a heart," Lilium uttered quietly.

"Is this wrong? Do others not?"

"Few, if any of the others do. I feel that they enjoy the hunt. Perhaps that is why so many are called to the Fey Wilde so soon."

"You?"

"Good intention and duty. I feel, but I do not regret my path. One day I will join the Fey Wilde and I will be at ease of my burdens when I am in that beauty."

"Me?"

Lilium smiled and the dread between them seemed thinner. "The weight of regret means that you are good. If I knew that I could give you your freedom from this path I would give it to you and then you might find a better life for a time before joining me again in the Fey Wilde."

Terica closed her eyes and tried to remember the times she had seen the realm beyond her visions. "And then I can be beside Vanessa in her wood."

The smiles faded and the dread of the weapon returned. Lilium felt herself become anxious again and she leaned on her companion as she tried to ward away the dark feelings. "Tell me of your dream once more and we shall try to interpret it again."

CHAPTER XVII
ARRIVING TO OVELCLUTCH

After leaving the borders of the Ash Wood the three had met the Imperial Marching Road and began south. It was a well-cared for highway of the Empire, comfortable underfoot, built on a foundation of stones and packed with good sands. They were quiet often around the cart and Basimick tried to keep his sight away from his woods and mountains. To the west was a wide grassland, flat and endless to the horizon which he stared at throughout the day. At night there were no lights, but a dim haze of civilization dimmed the stars south toward the end of the road.

They made camp on the east side of the Marching Road and Cassius could see Basimick looking at the glow to the south. "Ovelclutch," Cassius smiled at the haze. "Won't be long now, just another morning perhaps and we will have the evening to explore."

"Just the evening? Last time we were there you needed a few nights to explore the markets," Longinus laughed. He leaned to Basimick and offered some of his ration, a dry bit of jerky that was tough and stale, "Anytime we enter a dwarf city he takes a bit."

"I just want to see what they have."

"He wants to be adopted, I think. Learn their forges, trade their tart fruits, and eat their roasts. He would have liked to have been born a dwarf."

"Lived around them enough back near dwarf country," Cassius nodded. "Liked their mountains better than tilling the farms."

The two hunters kept chatting until they all fell asleep for the night, though anytime they thought they had an opportunity they offered Basimick a chance to enter the conversation, but he remained lost in his own thoughts until he also fell asleep. There were few words exchanged as they packed their camp the next morning and Basimick kept his eyes on the grasslands before Longinus leaned over, "Elves live out there."

"Elves," Basimick squinted to see if he could see any sign of them.

"Plain elves," Longinus whispered. "They live on that side of the road. That's their border and they seem to know if you cross it. The Empire had some trouble with them an Age ago, not a great moment for the Empire mind you, but the elves out there won their right to live as they do in a big war and now travelers stick to the roads."

Basimick shook his head and stared away from the grasslands, "There are a lot of wars."

"History is full of sad tales, lad. Forget that I mentioned it."

They continued south on the Marching Road and Cassius shouted as the glare of the city came into view. "There it is! That palace, I see it, all shiny in the sun." The cart began to move at a quicker pace as Cassius' excitement urged him onward. "Take a look! Take a look at it!"

The city was grand and coated in iron tiles so that the towers and walls were rusting into a deep red hue. The armor tiles were managed by the skill of the dwarves so that the rusting occurred with beautiful purpose. On the rooftops were details of shining gold vanes and copper shingles that were each kept pristine so that they shone brightly in the sunlight as a beacon for summoning travelers in all directions. The three moved southward down the Imperial Marching Road that met at the gates of the city, which was only one of the great roads that all met at the Courtyard of the Keep in the very center of Ovelclutch.

Basimick was in the back of the cart as Cassius switched the yolk with Longinus for his shift to pull. He looked at the city through tired eyes and it delivered only hope of food to him, but it gave no solace or comfort for his woes.

"Be mindful of your tone here, lad. We come to the great southern trade hub, Ovelclutch. It is owned by the dwarves of Helena's Cradle, you know, and managed well too. It is a powerful ally to the Empire." Cassius looked at the city with wonder. "Wish I could see Arrumklad, I do. They say it is a great dwarf city built out of the greatest mountain to have ever graced Nhearn. Places like that have deeper histories than even our Empire does, perhaps."

Longinus laughed, "I would like to see it too, save for the mountain trails sure to be about. Bit too up in the clouds for pulling a cart all that way."

"A dream is a dream," Cassius sighed.

The trio arrived near the city's northern gateway which housed an iron portcullis that was maintained and kept shining so that there was no sign of the city's rust decorum upon it. It was the very symbol of a stalwart defender, powerful in its own right, built for the peace and protection of the city. The gate house that restrained the metal bars was decorated red with rust and its foundation was red from heavy iron brick. The iron bars of the portcullis were kept well into the midsection of the immense gatehouse, reached by way of a tunnel whose height could fit two of Basimick's homes. "There were dwarves in Kurrum," He said. "But I did not see anything so...so-"

"Impressive," Cassius smiled.

"You should see the Imperial cities too," Longinus added. "There are many things I am sure you have missed sitting in your village." He meant it nicely and Basimick tried to shrug off the thought of the fire in his home as best he could. Instead he let his mind drift away in awe of the city, but he swayed back at times to his love for the sight of the Ash Mountains in the distance and the woodlands in the foothills.

They entered the tunnel and it echoed so that their voices were doubled in volume. As they approached the shining iron gate two dwarves armed with sizable axes stood to block their way. They wore armor of the city's deep red color, but despite the addition of rust, the armor looked like a formidable wall of metal protecting the stout long beards. "Hold there and state your cause."

Cassius presented the sigil coin of his position and the guards nodded.

"Be kind here, master hunters. I feel a storm coming."

"Honor the rock," Cassius said reluctantly.

"Honor the stone," replied the dwarves in unison and the gate opened with a repetitive clanking of machinery overhead in the gatehouse.

Cassius smiled and gave a wink to Longinus who smiled back knowing how ecstatic it must have been for his companion to be honored with dwarven custom.

As they entered the city proper, Basimick found himself out of sorts, and nervous even, by the large crowds. Throngs of dwarves went about their day through the market stalls and in the many smitheries were dwarves displaying their craft. Overhead was a heavy cloud of the daily routine as flumes built into the rusty towers let the smoke eject in all directions from beautifully carved chimneys. Humans too wandered the streets and purchased all manner of dwarven makes with Imperial sovereigns that were eagerly accepted by the dwarven shopkeepers.

"I have never seen so many people before," Basimick whispered. "I would not have guessed that there could be so many."

"It's not all that busy today. Amnith, our Empire's throne city, may have just as many in at least half the space," Longinus answered.

The trio dragged their cart through the street and it shook violently over the cobblestone. They moved down the main road, a wide mall flanked to either side by tall rusty abodes and in the street were stalls where vendors sold all manner of wear from the four corners of Nhearn. The road from the gate went straight and met the midwall where the inner district acted as a defensible vault. Dwarven banks, trade organizers, and envoys of the dwarven kingdoms stayed within the inner district. The main road continued through the open midgate and it could be seen that the center gates too were opened. There at the heart of the city was a fortress tower, a dome of iron, polished and neat, where below, in the Iron Park, the roads all converged at four cardinal gateways. Through these open doors the opposite side of the city could be seen, through the banks of the southern portion of the inner district, into the markets of the outer district, and to the iron tunnel of the southern gate house

where the Imperial Marching Road continued toward
Southrunn.

Basimick stayed near the cart of weapons and no
one within the city bothered them. Between the three
hunters and everyone else was a wide clearance. He
peeked around at the crowds and it seemed there were
several humans in a heated debate within the markets
nearing the gates. From the road south was a man
dressed in the sigils of Southrunn, his lordly clothes
giving him a regal flare, and across from him was a man
in the markings of Midland who had come from the
northern road. Between them both was a dwarf who
attempted to plan their marches. His thick finger had a
tattoo of a dwarvish rune on it and he used it to point at
the outer districts. "Both armies 'll pass, one of 'em to
the east and one of 'em to the west. Both 'll have to go
through the outer markets. South 'll pass and 'ead north,
and north 'll pass and 'ead south."

"So be it," and the Imperial speakers shook hands.

"An important gateway," Cassius explained after
noticing Basimick watching the interaction. "This place
is a very important crossroad for most of Nhearn, but the
dwarves were clever to build the markets." Cassius
waved his hand to either side of the cart to show
Basimick the Outer Ring. It wrapped around the city and
he could see that markets were set in plenty to either
side of the wide road. "If you get caught needing to
wander through the ring they are sure to peddle
something before you reach the other side. The dwarven
kingdoms from all Nhearn know the stories about the
wealth that trades hands here. This home knows all the
paths, though dwarves are sure to hide their deepest
secrets."

"Why are they so secretive," Basimick asked.

"Oh, most people are," Cassius hadn't bothered before with such a thought. "The dwarven mountains have secret roads, the elven woods have secret paths, the orc in their lands hold a few secrets too, and even us humans can vault a secret or two away."

"Of course we would have to come at a time when the armies are passing through," Longinus sighed as they made some distance across the mall of the main road. "Guess we will have some extra spans to walk through the market to the other side now."

"If there is an army marching through Ovelclutch, the whole city shuts the inner gates," Cassius pointed to the midgate where the road divided the city in half. The dwarf gave a shout up to the guards in the inner gatehouse and a horn sounded which was answered by several others throughout the inner ring.

Longinus tried to stretch beneath the yolk of the cart, "Now we will have to walk the outer market ring all the way around."

Cassius smiled over to Longinus, "Little blessings."

Longinus pulled the yolk and turned the cart toward the western edge of the outer ring. "Some would say you wished for this, old friend."

In the markets most people wandered about, buying and selling, imperial sovereigns trading hands, yet still none dared to approach the three of them, a surprise to Basimick who saw the aggressive fervor of the merchants toward passersby. An imperial soldier was the only one who neared them along their way. He was uniformed with the legion sigils of Southrunn, but he was not geared yet for war, and he faced Cassius before bowing. The soldier said nothing but Cassius waved a salute and the soldier went back to his *off duty* shopping.

Basimick looked at his hunter's token, "I didn't know the dragon hunters were part of the Imperial military."

"We aren't," Longinus laughed. "Soldiers respect us though. There are few offices that the Emperor controls directly and even the Legion pays its respects when they appear."

"Not everyone could do the duty of the Emperor's bidding," Cassius said to Longinus. He looked over to Basimick, "But I respect the soldiers. Not everyone could do that either."

"Where are they heading? Are they going to Kurrum?"

Cassius frowned, "I do not think so, lad."

"What would two armies be doing out here?"

"Orc, I would guess. There is enough trouble along the borders with the orc, has been for as long as I've been alive, and further back than that too." Cassius thought about the question a moment, "They might be refreshing ranks on the borders. Southrunn sends soldiers up to assist Midland and they send new recruits for training at the Imperial Legion forts back near the capital. They must have just been passing through on the Marching Road between here and there."

Basimick then spotted an elf within the market and about them were other elves that did not make a purchase or bother to look about the stalls. They refused the market and stood well away from others.

"Yo, elf, where ye be headin'?" A city guard approached them and demanded an answer.

"We came to pass through."

"Ye stayed long enough, I think. We will be needin' the gates to close and ye best pass on through unless ye intend on the stayin' toll. We ain't a castle for ye and yers."

The elves looked to one another and then one asked, "The gates are closing for the Imperial armies?"

"Aye." The dwarf pointed to the gate, "And ye need to be movin'."

"When will the gates reopen," another elf asked. "We hope to return to the markets without interference from the Empire of Man."

"When ye see 'em open, they be open."

The elves left toward the eastern gates, walking out of view along the curved path of the city, talking amongst themselves in their own tongue and avoiding the vendors who still tried to get any coins they might have had.

Cassius saw Basimick staring elsewhere, "See anything you like, lad?"

"No," he said grimly. "Back home there was an elf who said they didn't like dwarves. It seemed the dwarves didn't like her either."

Longinus glanced at Basimick and tried to spot what he had been watching. "They live a long time. I've heard elves can live for a millennium."

"Dwarves can live to be over five centuries if I remember right," Cassius added.

"It takes a long time for ideas to change when you have all that lifetime to remember what happened, and then your forebears are not far from deeper wounds than that." Longinus shrugged, "Humans, we don't last too long in the grand scheme of things."

They moved through the markets still unbothered and as the western midgate became imposing a dwarf rushed out to the middle of the road to stand in their way. He wore a woven tunic of shimmering silk in a rust color with a belt of fine suede buckled with gold. His beard was well groomed, waxed and curled below his chin to form tusks where clasps of copper rings kept the display in check. On his chest was an iron bar hung by a necklace, the polish plainly showing a royal crest of Ovelclutch. "Hold there, master hunters," he bowed as low as he could without the metal on his face tipping him off balance. "Word has spread like a wildfire in the plains that you entered the northern gate house. You are not just passing through I would hope, for the Trade Master would very much like your company."

Cassius looked at the other two, longing in his eyes, and Basimick gave his best smile while nodding with approval. Longinus grinned, knowing that to dissuade the invitation would likely leave him pulling the cart the rest of the trip on his own. "As you wished for, friend."

"We would gladly accept an invitation from the Trade Master," Cassius bowed back.

The dwarf smiled and nodded incessantly. "Understandably we are to make haste, given your role. Do not think that you are just Imperials now," the dwarf laughed from deep in his gut. "The Trade Master wishes me to tell you that your duties are to the greater benefit of all Nhearn. You do the good works of protecting all good folks. I thank you myself too. Would you accept an invitation to tonight's dinner feast?"

"Absolutely," Cassius was beaming.

"I have been given permission also to offer you lodging within the halls of the Iron Keep. Do not let the hard exterior fool you, it is quite comfortable."

"Of course, we would be happy to accept such royal accommodations."

"What about the cart? I wouldn't trust it to be out of our sight near the markets," Longinus attempted to whisper.

"Do not insult our host," Cassius also tried to whisper.

"No fear, dragon hunters. I would not risk your devices to the pilfering of common vendors. No smith or coin trader will lay a finger on it and shy from consequence when such nobility is in question. However, to avoid such fuss as to entice the vagrants from a prize like your own, allow the Iron Keep to host your wares also." The dwarf waved into the hall of the midgate and from within arrived four guards adorned in rust colored armor that still shined in the sun with the polished character of quality iron. "Allow them to take your burden to safety. The inner vaults of our castle will be as yours while you are guests in this house."

"Many thanks," Cassius' smile returned to his face. Longinus too gave a great smile as the dwarven guard relinquished him of the yolk to take up the handles of their heavy cart. "Will you lead the way?"

The host pointed for the guard to take the cart ahead of them and they moved so quickly so that Basimick gave some reservations to the shaking cargo against the cobblestone. "We shall go at once to the keep. I am sure your travels have kept you away from good food and crisp water. We will fill you kindly here."

The inner city was less open than the market ring. There were many avenues dividing the tall red towers from each other so that the inner ring was like a maze to the uninitiated. Casting shadows from above were bridges and stairways between each of the towers so that the city was layered upon itself. Dwarves met with one another in the upper heights of the city, atop the buildings where parks had been created to rest in the sun, and within the towers were halls lit by braziers to conduct the business of the trade hub.

The host continued along the main road toward the innermost gate where the color of the city vanished to the pristine metal palette of polished iron. "Here you will stay with us in the Iron Keep," the host waved their hands to show the wonder of the dome that protected the heart of the city. "Our most esteemed masters of Ovelclutch reside here and you are welcome as equals. Allow me to show you to your accommodations for the time being."

The lower chambers of the Iron Keep were more than comfortable and the three of them found themselves relaxing without much effort. The dwarven servants of Ovelclutch made sure that the hunters had been given new clothes, time to clean themselves from travel in the baths, and they were allowed time undisturbed to rest from their aches before their summons for the feast. They had spent much of the afternoon sleeping but a knock at the door by their host had woken them in time to prepare for the evening dinner. They all got dressed and Cassius was wearing a wide smile as he inspected himself in a tall mirror. He had polished his boots, cleaned his jacket, and then selected a sword with a glimmering hilt fit for pleasant company.

"You are trying too hard, old friend."

"Not every day you get invited to dine with royalty, aye lad?"

Basimick nodded but he couldn't stand staring at his reflection. He had slept some, mostly from being tired, but even then his nerves could not allow his body to rest or his thoughts to silence, and he spent the brief sleep restless. He watched Cassius admire himself and Basimick looked at his sleeves. They were clean now where his old shirt had been dirty with soot from his failed attempts to rescue anyone. The grime and smell that he began to notice before the baths was gone and his body was washed from dirt and exertion, but he did not feel clean from the guilt in his stomach. He returned his gaze to Cassius' happy moment but his head sunk low into thoughts of Kurrum once again.

"Here," Longinus sat beside him on the comfortable couch. "It is a genuine dragon jacket. Imperial made. Had to think of the right size before I had it pulled from our cart for you."

"I couldn't," Basimick denied it humbly.

"Who could, Basimick," Cassius said, still looking at his most pompous self.

Longinus shook the uniform at him. "Did you not strike, with your own hand, the great Olag of Fire, a dragon so fierce that death itself is afraid to claim that soul?"

"I did, but I was afraid-"

"I was afraid too," Longinus gently patted Basimick on the back. "Yet I only shot at the beast," he added with a laugh. "A few hits in at a distance, of course."

Basimick allowed a smile to slip through his despair, "I suppose I did get closer than you."

"Take it. No one deserves it more."

He took it and held it up. It was a happy moment that caught him wandering away from his darker thoughts of failing to slay Olag like he planned and the wrath he brought onto Kurrum for his decision. It was a heavy leather jerkin that had been just polished so that the texture of scales which decorated the whole outfit appeared to shine. He put on the new dragon hunter's uniform and cinched it as tight as he could. It fit near perfectly.

"The leather will loosen a bit with use," Cassius patted his own jacket that matched with Longinus and Basimick. "But it looks grand, all new and clean. Perfect time to break it in, aye lad?" Basimick nodded and felt like he could see into the mirror, but as he got close he shied away.

"You look good," Longinus said, hoping to comfort Basimick, for it had taken him a long time to find solace in his own thoughts too. "Just for comfort though, I find it best to keep this here looser." Longinus fidgeted with a buckle near the hips. "Lets you twist a bit more when the need comes."

"Thank you."

"You look the part now," Cassius nodded proudly. "Matches with your deeds."

Basimick went to the pile of his old clothes and pulled the coin out of the pocket of his old shirt. As he set the clothes down Cassius came and handed Basimick a sigil pendant. He looked at the pair of them who both pointed to the left shoulder clasp where their own pendants were shown with honor. He went to set it and struggled with puncturing it through the new leather for a moment. "How is this?"

"Perfect, master hunter," Cassius pretended to wipe a tear from his eye.

"If you wanted to just take a peek," Longinus feigned a smile.

"I think I might try to see." Basimick stepped in front of the tall mirror, his head low so that he could see the shine of the new boots offered to him by their host. He slowly raised his head up and found that the clean pants were a nice addition to the ensemble. He thought for a moment that he must have looked like a vagrant that the real hunters rescued from a wretched village somewhere out in the Badlands. His gaze continued up and he admired the jacket that was molded to look like he had dragon scales across his torso. At his waist was the sword his father had given him, still polished and pristine so that it was even more presentable than Cassius' show sword. He continued and the pendant of the dragon hunter was worn with honor over the left shoulder clasp. He was stricken with a moment of pride before continuing to his own eyes. *Would my father be proud of me?* The thought came to him immediately. Basimick stared at his eyes in the reflection for what seemed like a long moment, but it only took an instant for him to flee from his own gaze.

"It looks good, yes," Longinus was hopeful that he didn't force the young boy into facing anything too early.

"It looks fit for a royal feast," Basimick nodded and forced a smile while restraining himself from tears.

"Let's drown it all out with good food for the night," Cassius swept Basimick under his arm as another knock came to their door. "I think you are ready to eat. I know I am."

As Cassius opened the door a dwarf in fine rust colored armor entered the room. "Something has happened, master hunters. You will excuse the Trade Master for the moment, but I have been tasked with taking you to safety."

Longinus hurriedly grabbed a few items of importance before heading toward the dwarf at the door, "What happened?"

"Time to reflect on what happened will come. Now is the time to get yourselves to safety. The inner ring and the hold of the Iron Keep have several covered streets dug into the foundation for protection, fortress bunkers where you might be safe." The dwarf pounded his fist on his armor so that it rang loudly in the room. "Quickly, master hunters."

CHAPTER XVIII
THE FIRST MOVE OF THE ELVES

Agnithia Witch-Heart sat and waited for the Imperial armies to pass and the gates of Ovelclutch to reopen. They spent most of the morning gathering in the eastern hills beyond the sight of the city while several scouts had gone ahead to give a signal when the Imperial Legion had moved onward. As they returned to the forces of the Sentinel Woods they reported the departure of both human forces. "We were also allowed to venture into the markets before the gates had shut for the humans."

Agnithia waited silently as her lieutenants considered the matter. The dark shaeman smiled, "I have told you, they suspect nothing."

One of the lieutenants reiterated the plan to the others, "Move all into position at the eastern gate by way of the road. Tell them we are returning to Krethnarok from the Forbidden Lands. We will enter the city as though we mean no harm to explore the markets."

"Dwarves believe we are not to be trusted," one of the lieutenants added. He was an elf of a noble stratum and was not afraid to offer their opinion, "We have fought too many wars with them to walk through unsuspectedly."

"Not these ones," the dark shaeman interjected. "These ones are merchants. Our scouts entered, perhaps with a bit more attention than the humans, but they entered just the same. These dwarves will want us to pass through their city instead of around in the grassland."

The noble elf scoffed, "And why is that?"

Agnithia hissed at the elf of high status who was denying the efficacy of their plans, "The time has come." She handed a heavy sack to them and pointed at the dwarven gate. "Begin the toll," the order came from beneath the metal of her mask. The lieutenant opened the satchel and found within it a treasury of gold that must have been taken from the royal homes in the Sentinel Woods. "They will be bribed to their doom," she pointed and sent the others to oversee their forces while the one holding the sack was sent ahead to the city.

Throughout the evening her army swelled, ranks of elves nearing the eastern gate of the city, the road filling with a battalion of her armed soldiers preparing to pass through the market streets of Ovelclutch. From the west came an elven horn blast announcing that another army had arrived at the dwarven city to pay toll through the western gate on the same road opposite her forces.

"It shall be the forces of Hissilanda the White coming from Krethnarok," Agnithia told the shaeman as they waited for the noble elf to deal with the gate. "This shall be swift."

"The shadow of Maribel protects our secrets, my lady."

The elf of high position went forth from the waiting army to meet with the eastern gate of Ovelclutch where the Imperial Way that wandered out to the Badlands met and passed through the city toward the western territories of the Empire. The gatehouse tower was immense and the tunnel seemed dark by its very length. At the first of three closed iron portcullis were two armored dwarves, each adorned in rusty iron armor and they wielded large pole axes. "Speak in the Imperial Common there, elf lord?"

The elf twisted their face at the request, "That it is considered the common of Nhearn is the hubris of that Empire."

"Aye, let's ye and me talk though. I'd preferin' a common than ne'er say 'ello to gate walkers." The dwarf guard looked to see the army amassing behind the guest. "Passin' through?"

"We travel west to Krethnarok from the Sentinel Woods."

"Issues in the Badlands?"

"Perhaps, but my business is of elvenkind."

"So be it," the dwarf added kindly. "Move on toward the right, then circle the outer ring north till ye reach the western gate. The far side will take ye to yer friendly woodland." The dwarf held out his hand.

"To tax us and then expect us to wander your markets," the elf spat. With frustration a sizable tax of elven gold was given over to the gate's guard.

The second guard then pulled upon a rope hidden beside the guard post so that high above in the gate tower was a ringing bell that began a series of clanking gears and a movement of thundering weights. The iron bars lifted and the tunnel was open for the army to pass. The elven lead took a horn to his lips and the sound echoed into the hills off of the city wall. All at once the elven army gathered in line and entered the city of Ovelclutch.

Where the dwarf guards stood, hidden within the tunnel passage in a nook carved into the tunnel wall, was a metal pipe that ran the height of the tower. A voice came through the metal tube to speak with the hidden guard, "Dreggo-Gatewatcher, get this elven host movin'. Another lot of 'em just entered through the west gates headin' east."

"Mangred, tell the inner gate to shut. Hold 'em in the markets a bit," and Dreggo put the toll into a bucket dumbwaiter that was taken up into the gatehouse vaults earnestly.

From each of the opposite gates were vast elven armies, each encircling the outer market ring, marching toward the gates farthest across the city. They marched diligently, not one elven soldier answering the hollers of the dwarven market vendors. The cardinal doors into the inner district were closed, a common practice while armies moved through, and the elves began to fill up the outer ring's roadway as their leaders halted before the intermediate gates which held the forces still as the other army passed onward. "Why is the way closed," the head elf called up nervously to the dwarven gate master who stood above the halted army upon the bridge between the outer ramparts and the inner wall above the markets.

"Army passin' yonder. Tis nearin' the end soon and the inter gate will open."

The lieutenant waited at the gate and the two dwarven guards protecting the portcullis watched him carefully. "Enjoying the markets, elf master?"

"I saw nothing," the elf tried to think of how to speak in the common tongue.

"Not practiced in Imperial? Must not come 'round much. Sure is a lot to look at. Are you sure you saw nothing you liked?"

The lieutenant did not reply, choosing to wait for the gate to open in silence, but their posture was swaying and nervous. None of the other elves behind the leader broke rank, each one standing stalwart as center to the ring as they could, and none of them shifted to look at any of the vendors begging for their attention, whether to sell to them or from offers to purchase any elven trinkets they may have brought with them.

One of the guards nodded to the other before departing into a guard nook embedded into the wall of the intermediary gatehouse. He spoke his language into the metal pipe to the gate master, "Something odd about this one. What army is passing yonder?"

"Elves too."

"Best see Rongar Battle-Master and let him know we got two elven armies at once."

"They've been less mad 'bout moving 'bout the city than the Imperials this mornin'. You've been listenin' to your pa rantin' the old days again after 'is tavern meet?"

"Not about hating elves, gate master. Just thought it odd, this one."

There was a pause from the gate master before asking the guard, "You sure?"

"I don't like the way this army is passing," the guard said. "Rather the battle master knew about it."

The other guard at the gate looked up as a sound hit his ears from a distance. "Not a tower horn. Aye, what is that," he turned into the guard's nook and asked his companion what the noise was from.

"You heard that," the guard called up into the metal tube.

No answer came but a crashing noise clattered onto the street of the gate. The pair of guards turned from the nook and saw that the gate master had fallen from above, an elven arrow shaft accurately struck him in the head where he had been unhelmed at his post. The elf no longer seemed nervous as they lowered their bow and blew upon a horn to answer the sound that had arisen from the other side of the city.

All at once the elves drew weapons and the market ring became an instant horror. Dwarves who were unaware were excited to have the elven soldiers come near, expecting trade or purchase, but the razor edged blades of the elves cut through cloth and flesh with ease. Along the wall, where guards kept an eye on the market road below, the elves brought death and the stationed dwarves were suddenly struck by deadly biting arrows from all around them. Some who were unfortunate enough to survive being struck during the ambush fell from the heights of the ramparts and the heavy iron armor crumpled around them as they landed upon the stone streets beneath their perch. The outer ring was a flurry of violence. Vendors, workers, citizens, and visitors were all caught by surprise and none were treated any differently in the eyes of the elves. In moments the city was quelled, the outer ring, the market road, and the outer wall were all captured.

The elves gathered at the stairs and filled the ramparts with archers who fired across the market chasm at the inner ramparts where dwarven warriors retreated into the city defenses of the inner wall. Battles across the intermediate gate bridges allowed elven skirmishers to reach the ramparts upon the inner side where they clashed with the few soldiers that the dwarves could muster in short notice. Those who discovered the danger early enough fled into the inner district through passages above the markets, near the upper levels of the wall, and the guards waited as long as they could before closing the way between the vault district and the outer city.

From the tall wall of the second ring of the city the dwarven guards stationed themselves to operate large ballistae meant to fire into the fields beyond the outer wall. Their strong arms twisted on cranks that pulled the cords tight and flung long javelins at the outer ramparts where the elven archers had begun to gather. They turned the machine over and over, the springs and levers clicking new spears into the weapon, but it was not quick enough to outpace the many archers in the elven ranks. A barrage of elven arrows swarmed each defensive tower as the turrets revealed themselves in their attempt to defend the city.

"Search all the passages," the lieutenant ordered. "Witch-Heart wants none left alive."

The elves began to destroy the stalls scattered along the wide market road to find any who had chosen to hide beneath their counters. They entered into the alleyways between the forges and dwellings to seek any dwarf who had fled too late to the gates that had now been closed to protect the passages to the inner rings. As groups of elves hunted deeper into the halls and homes of the city the mass of the battalion gathered upon the inner and outer ramparts flanking the market ring.

"Let loose! Worry not of the waste; worry only that they might live! Deliver death to them! Remove them from this world! For Vanessa, slay them all!" At their command all the elves prepared their bows and strung their arrows to volley. As the battalion began to attack the inner ring the message was sent to further elven warriors along the market rampart. From every direction of the outer ring the arrows were let loose and in waves they began to strike the copper rooftops of the inner city.

Dwarves atop the inner wall retreated as the parapets above were cracked by arrows in the thousands. The iron tiled walls sparked as elven archers relentlessly unleashed themselves upon Ovelclutch, driving the soldiers and guards of the city deeper inward.

CHAPTER XIX
HIDING

At the top of the Iron Keep was a ring for the Trade Master to view the lanes of traffic within the city. He had a crowd gathered trying to make sense of what had happened and many voices were begging for action as the screams of the outer ring began to silence. He stroked his braided beard and remained silent as the arrows of the elves began to appear below and ring on the metal shingles of the inner city. In his mind the city of Ovelclutch had high walls clad in metal with foundations of stone, it was as impenetrable as the mountains, built to last as a kingdom just as any other dwarven home before it, but the elven army was not holding back.

"What are we to do, Trade Master?"

At last their leader spoke, "We must send messengers to the other holds that the elves have attacked."

"There is no way out to send word," one shouted as they circled the top of the Iron Keep to witness how coordinated the elves had been in sealing their passage.

The noble dwarves looked at the districts to the north where the city had a clear line dividing the buildings out to the northern gate house of the Marching Road. Within the outer ring of the city were elves numbering in the thousands, a massive force capable of

194

rivaling the Imperial forces of Southrunn. Beyond the wall another force was arriving, hidden in the grasses until they revealed themselves on the Marching Road. They were the plain elves of the Great Plains, more numerous than any could have predicted.

As the nobles continued in circles they could see that yet more of the elves were arriving from the east, armies brought under black flags of the Sentinel Woods, and as they revealed their numbers on the Imperial Way hope began to diminish entirely. To the south were yet more elves, groups of the nomads from the vast valley lands who could move with stealth through the grass.

"How could they have gotten so close to the city without the towers of Argenkul seeing this?"

Another dwarf answered from among the nobles, "Magics, as elves do. They can move like shadows out there, damn grass walkers. The towers probably never saw a hair on them."

The Trade Master knew what was to come as they continued along the balcony ring atop the Iron Keep. The western gate had been taken by the elven battalions that were allowed to enter the city, but beyond the walls was another force coming from the ancient elven land of Krethnarok. The Trade Master leaned against the balcony to the west and the other dwarves grew worried. "These elves are a different lot," he uttered quietly with dread.

They displayed white banners of Queen Hissilanda the White which were held aloft with silver metal instead of the usual elven banners held by wood and colored with the hue of the season. The elves among the ranks of that force were well armed, well supplied, and although they were outnumbered by their companion forces, they were each as deadly and as experienced as a score of Imperial soldiers in lifespan alone.

"What are we to do?"

"They have taken the outer ring, they have control of every gate, and now the market is quiet except the orders those elves mutter in their forest tongues. It is too late to send word; even our swiftest dwarves would have issue crossing through all these elven lines now. They came in and paid the toll did they not? They were welcomed inside weren't they?"

"What of the Empire? The legion is not far?"

"I can't see the humans on the road now," the Trade Master closed his eyes. "They waited for the Imperials to leave. It's between us and them then. So much for a few centuries at peace."

Down below within the inner city the dwarves continued to shout at each other, giving other bands news if their gates were holding or if repairs were needed. Forge tenders who had survived the markets offered their skills to seal the doors closed with additional metals, their hammers working to drive rivets into metal beams to brace them all shut. Brave soldiers hid behind the parapets along the wall above the inner pathways and called out times when the archers in the outer ring were lessening the volley or were focused on the ballista turrets in hopes that groups of survivors could make for safety at the interior bunker safes.

"Battle Master," one of the soldiers keeping watch on the volley, caught the attention of the city defense leader. "The survivors need to go now, and you need to tell the Trade Master what is happening!"

Rongar Battle-Master nodded and limped to the group of dwarves hiding within the tunnel between the ramparts of the rings. His shield arm hung limp but still strapped to it was his heavy iron shield. In his other was an axe adorned with the runes of his position and with a wave of the weapon the dwarves rushed out of the tunnel into the inner city. Rongar moved quickly, gritting his teeth from the wounds, and he led the group into the interior of a banking hall to duck for cover.

Another volley rose into the sky and all about the edges of the inner ring the arrows fell like rain. From the banking hall Rongar looked to the sky for another opening in the attack. He could see other faces in windows within the towers around his position. There were bodies scattered along the balconies and bridges, within the streets and rooftop parks. None that had lingered outside were safe and even trained soldiers stayed trapped indoors as they waited for breaks in the assault to retrieve more groups of survivors from the wall. Against the metal shingles few arrows held, but the sound was in the likeness of a thousand smithy strikes and it did not leave room for a peaceful thought among his group.

"Now, with haste!" Again they ran, Rongar limping down stairwells to get to the streets below. He waved his axe to those fleeing in front of him and led them down the labyrinth toward the old doors that only the city guard still knew about. At last, before another deadly hail of arrows stormed through the city again, they reached a large door that seemed to share a likeness to other dwellings nearby. The Battle Master was pulled on by several who lifted him from his wounded leg and he was brought to the door where the pommel of his axe found purpose. He shoved it into a hole in the brick beside the door, perfect for the pole size of his axe, and he twisted it like a key, releasing dust from the seal of the door.

All at once the dwarves pushed each other into the old room. It was filled with dust and old crates of dried supplies which may have spoiled long before. "Go deeper in," Rongar ordered them down the incline of the chamber. "The way goes beneath the Iron Keep and hides underground. We will be safe from the arrows here."

"I hear voices," one of the dwarves panicked.

The door shut and the mechanisms clanged together as the locks snapped together to seal the passage. "More survivors," Rongar told them. "There is another vault door as we near the Iron Keep should we need to enter the Iron Park for safety," and the group followed him deeper into the dark tunnel vault beneath the city.

Rongar Battle-Master, the city's watch captain, now entered the bunker room of the inner ring through a pair of the Iron Keep's guard. About him were many that he had already saved, but some were not so grateful for it. They looked at him as Rongar-Watchman, pained with disgust and shame. Even Rongar himself walked with his head held low, for he thought that he alone had failed the city. An army had come, and another, and more also until he had what must be all of the elven armies in Nhearn amassed within the city he was charged with protecting.

"You shall be Rongar-Exiled should we ever be free again," and from a throng of fearful dwarves came a red fruit that splattered against the armor of a guard unlucky enough to be standing beside Rongar.

One of the watchmen from the crowd drew out a blade, "If it weren't for him more would now lie dead. I saw, with his shield alone, he saved two scores of us. Had he not alarmed us, would ye not still be at yer own merchant's stall?"

From the group against the wall opposite of the offenders, one dwarf stood up from the crowd and shouted over the murmuring noise, "I'd been a pin cushion, I would, with an elven barb, had the guards not have found me. They deserve our thanks!"

"Hoorah," some shouted and raised their arms high into the air. "Honor to Rongar, honor to the guard!"

"How many are dead?" A dwarf leapt between the throngs into the middle of the bunker street and stood before the passing group of guards gathering around Rongar for orders. "How many are our losses?"

"Quiet Olpho, less you lose your Miller and become Olpho-Pigheaded!"

"Who would ask then, aye? It weighs on us all," the miller cried back. "Rongar?"

"I would not count our loss while the arrows yet fell. A fool's errand to count such a thing while more lives may be saved." Rongar at last lifted his head up. "Let us instead find a way to end this before we lose the city altogether."

The clinking of armor from deeper along the bunker street hushed the crowd's murmuring. "Soldiers."

It was a statement made flatly and boldly at the hulking dwarf who stood there in the heaviest plates the armory could manage to forge. "Call for the reserve armies of Argenkul," the hulking dwarf ordered.

Rongar nodded to the lead soldier, "It is nice to see you alive and well, Karn Battle-Master. I would call your garrison if they were not far beyond the walls and the gates were not overrun."

Karn moved forward to pass the protective guard line around Rongar and they moved away from his path to let him near the city's Battle Master out of respect for the soldier's status. "We will not hold long in battle. A siege we might, perhaps, for your city stores are well managed, but if those gates fall-"

"We must hold the gates and keep our hope. You and I, Karn, with the Trade Master of the city, we must all make a plan." The two of them walked on, continuing together side by side through the throngs of dwarves and refugees as the crowds began to raise their voices again in restless chatter.

Amidst the gatherings, among the nooks built in case this hall needed to be defended, were the three of them; Basimick, Cassius, and Longinus. "What have you heard, Cassius? I cannot speak dwarvish."

"Me either," Basimick added, a bit embarrassed for having lived beside a dwarven mine his whole life.

Cassius leaned around the corner and tried to see if any important members were present, but the crowds had settled into their separate groupings and were once more in varied states of grief and fear. "I think they still have the inner city. At least the guard made it seem we did. There was some talk of reinforcements, but I don't know who they plan to call on. The Empire doesn't have a keep near here and the next dwarven city is high in the mountains southern and eastern from here. Could take near a week just to get a messenger that way, let alone time to mobilize an army."

Basimick leaned back into the wall and tried to get comfortable on the harsh stone of the bunker street. "What should we do to help?"

Longinus nodded at the thought of assisting, "We could lend our swords, but we are only three men after all."

Cassius leaned up next to Basimick, trying himself to get comfortable on the stony street. "Give me a bit of time and a target at least the size of three barns, then maybe I might help," he nudged Basimick with a light chuckle. "Not much use for a dragon lancer at the time."

Basimick looked at them both, "Are we to do nothing?"

There was another volley of arrows that the bunker could hear against the metal shingles in the streets above them. The dwarves around the hunters began to speculate if the elves had begun to bang upon the gates of the bunker but the arrows began to quell and the debate resumed of whether to be hopeful or hopeless.

Basimick couldn't understand them, but he could feel the terror in their voices. "Why are they doing this, Cassius?"

"The elves have always feuded with dwarves. It has been the way of things through the histories. They are both too different, you see. A tree cannot understand the rock, nor do the peaks see for the roots, if the metaphor translates."

Basimick listened as another wave of several thousand arrows rained over the copper shingles of the city dwellings in the inner districts above. "Violence like this-"

"Is hard to explain," Longinus whispered to mind the topic while more refugees wandered into the safety of the vault. "The Empire doesn't involve itself much in the politics of elves and dwarves. I remember when I was learning some of it at the Imperial Academy, when I was still a young lad, the elves disliked the dwarves for using the woods as resources and carving the stones. The elves enjoy the beauty of the world and the dwarves enjoy making beauty of it."

Cassius nodded, "And when I was trading up north with the dwarves we never dealt with elves. Isolationists mostly."

"There have been skirmishes between them too. Border things I would guess. Hard to tell where the mountains end and the woodlands begin," Longinus guessed. "This has been a while coming I fear. Much further than our lifetimes maybe."

Basimick was confused by the explanations of politics, trading, borders, and the idea of killing to justify such things. He hoped for a more simple answer and asked, "What would drive a whole race to war?"

Cassius shook his head at the young boy. "Why do you hunt the dragon?"

"Revenge," Basimick answered honestly.

"I don't know what happened. Maybe the elves ruined a mine, or maybe the dwarves spoiled a forest, but I feel that these elves are coming in on the tide of rage."

Basimick looked around the fortified street and saw the tears, the sorrow, and the confused anger as the dwarves were brought into the safety of the bunker vault. "These people here are innocent though, at least they aren't soldiers or looking to fight."

"That is the difference between dueling and warfare," Longinus added. "You and a dragon, me and another, but war does not see one and another. It sees all and them. There is always a price to vengeance in one way or another, and especially more so in warfare."

Basimick watched with sadness as the weeping people gathered about in the final sanctuary of Ovelclutch. "How can the price be spared?"

"Forgiveness," Cassius answered grimly.

CHAPTER XX
BREAKING OVELCLUTCH

Agnithia marched through the gate with the dark shaeman at her side and their servants quietly moved behind them. "There are none left near us," the shaeman looked up to the ramparts of the market ring and watched the elven warriors send volley after volley into the inner city. "They have been thorough and your lieutenants have followed your orders strictly."

"They have proven loyal to the cause of the white queen," Agnithia whispered. "They will prove the same when we enact our plans after this is over."

"You have been too successful I fear." The shaeman held out a hand and from their sleeve slipped a collection of dark beads. A servant quickly arrived to collect the rosary made of onyx from the shaeman's hand before it was loosened to the street. The servant bowed and then set to the inner halls and avenues of the outer district while uttering prayers to the goddess of shadow. "The white queen will seek your assistance to the end of this vengeance. It will offer us better opportunities for the future of the wood, but it will be a distraction that might delay our plans."

"Then we will continue to contend with the dwarves. We must not let her know of our plans after this. I would not wish to cross her and receive this type of retribution upon ourselves."

They continued through the street, the dark shaeman offering more rosaries to each of the servants as they passed heavier clusters of dwellings to search through. As the servants returned they would bow their heads and report, "There were none that the moon could find."

"Then there were none to find," the shaeman would gently wave a hand and the servants would be off to seek dwarves among new ruins of the city.

The outer ring of Ovelclutch was overtaken; the elven armies that had fooled the gates were melding into a unified force within the outer ring of the city. The intermediate gates of the market ring had been opened and seized, the stairs of the outer ramparts were taken, and the elves were positioned at every tunnel that led further into the city from the inner rampart. There were still several skirmishes as the higher wall of the inner city still had soldiers willing to defend Ovelclutch, but the market streets were now quiet and Agnithia began to ensure their goals.

As she encountered her leaders she gave them new orders which were given to any warrior not firing their bows upon the inner city from the ramparts. There were no doors of any dwelling that had been left closed, no room that had been left unsearched, and no dwarf that had been offered mercy. From houses and stalls the final screams of the discovered dwarven victims cried out through the alleys and rang up through the chimneys until they reached the ears of those still alive within the inner ring. Dwarven corpses were collected when their deeds were done and the elves dragged them into the street to be piled together in heaps. Fuel was easy to find within the market smithies and the massive pyres were set ablaze all throughout the city.

Agnithia Witch-Heart stood at the largest of the pyres which had bodies heaped among tapestries, art, tools, plate ware, decor, food, and any refuse that elves thought as dwarven in nature. It was a purge of everything so that the empty city would be confused with ruins and its history would become lost for guessing as generations who still knew withered into antiquity.

As the elven general seemed to watch the fire a lieutenant from the woodlands of Krethnarok approached her, nervous of the servants gathered about in black robes and dark paints with symbols entirely foreign of Vanessa. "Let us now begin trying to breach the gate," Agnithia's voice seemed to resonate in the air. "These fires will break the spirit of the remaining dwarves and they will beg for merciful death as we near the heart of their city."

The white queen's lieutenant nodded, "I have just the thing."

As they departed to prepare the sundering of the northern gate the dark shaeman smirked. Without motion Agnithia hissed, "What is it?"

"The young elf from Krethnarok, they have not left the woodlands before. I can smell it like springtime on them."

The fire seemed to rise with Witch-Heart's frustration. "Perhaps the queen knew who to put in charge of this assault after all."

Staged now within the plaza between the cardinal gates of the outer and inner rings, the invaders prepared themselves to press onward into the inner city through the north cardinal gate, the elven mages testing their usual means to gain entry. The sorcerers gathered in circles and whispered magic incantations to force the doors open, yet their words and energy were stolen from the air. The lieutenant from Krethnarok began to shout at them to try harder, becoming disappointed at the mage's for their failures. As they chanted, several of them began to succumb to fatigue and collapsed, their magic draining from their bodies to vanish into the still air of the market ring.

Agnithia moved to the north gate quietly, her presence either unnoticed or the horror of it forcing unfamiliar soldiers to shy away. "Fools," she hissed metallically from beneath her mask. "These are dwarven runes! They will rob you of the arcane and bleed your magic." She silenced the elven sorcerers from sapping their strength further and grabbed hold of the novice elf leader, "It is their honored defense against our magics since they cannot summon from the Winds for themselves. We must break the door instead."

"Break the gate?" The lieutenant was unsure, "The dwarves build in strength first."

"All things fall in time," Agnithia pointed to several soldiers and bid them to collect axes and picks to destroy the doors. "We only need one entry." With a hand she summoned the moon servant and the entourage of dark followers. "Find the weakest door of the city."

"Of course," the shaeman gently waved the servants to their task.

The lieutenant scowled at the masked general, "You would send those dark spell casters into the city? What use-"

"They are not devoted to the arcane as your sorcerers," Agnithia corrected the bold elf. "They are empowered by a divine source from a higher power. Their powers are not bound to the sapping stones of the dwarves."

As the black robed elves dispersed through the market ring the warriors began to heave axes against the doors. Some groups discovered heavy instruments while forming the pyres and began to batter the gates with rams. From all directions the inner city was being assaulted and even from above were volleys of arrows raining down throughout the district's streets, managing such distance as to strike the exterior of the iron dome of the center most keep. Smoke rose from the outer ring, and the whole city was enveloped in a heavy stinking cloud of death.

CHAPTER XXI
ESCAPING OVELCLUTCH

The doorway of the bunker opened again and the dwarven crowds silenced as another surge of survivors entered the safety of the underground vault. A guard led the way and Cassius could hear the dwarves beg them for any news. "They have been knocking at every door of the inter halls and the outer ring is completely lost." The guard was panicked along with the survivors and their nerve broke to tell the tale. "There is a foul smoke in the air out there. I fear the gates won't last much longer."

Arrows continued to rain down across the metal topped buildings of the inner ring. The guard who had come in with the new survivors began to tear as horns of the keep sounded and called for the guards to return to their duty. "I can't go back," they shouted. "I've seen too much, smelled too much."

Another guard who was organizing the bunker street to allow more survivors into the nooks of the vault broke away from his task and went to the other tearful guard. "Stay 'ere an' man the vault. I will be goin' to task with these 'ere elves." With a pat of a metal gauntlet on the rusty pauldron the brave guard went up the ramp and disappeared from the sight of the bunker.

The concussive sounds of pounding could be heard as the elves attempted to enter the protected district of the inner ring. A thunderous noise of another elven volley struck every shingle of the rooftop metals outside and the dwarves began to cry out in the bunker street that the vault door had been left open.

The guard dwarf who remained in the chamber made a hesitant motion to close the gate but Cassius quickly stood up and stood in front of the trembling dwarf. "Honor the rock," he offered his hand.

"Honor the stone," the guard looked up into Cassius' eyes and handed over the rune axe key. "Close it, will you?"

Cassius nodded and waved to his other two companions to come with him. They moved passed the crowds of fearful dwarves who stared to watch the dragon hunters pass by, several of them stood with an arm over their chest to offer thanks and respect. They traveled out of sight from the crowds and the nooks of the defensible bunker street but before them were the moans of those unable to go any further. Up to the vault door, littered upon the ramp to the underground, were dwarves who could no longer move and they struggled with their injuries. Several had perished from many arrows embedded within them and some had deep gashes where elven swords had struck. There were families crying atop one another, whimpering at the terrible violence without knowing what could be done.

The dragon hunters at last got to the door which had been left open by the returning warriors, the horns still calling for all available to return to the defense of the city. The arrows still rained down and rang on the metal of the city as they struck from above. Cassius peered out of the doorway and could see that not many were as lucky as the dwarves who had made it within the vault.

Basimick gazed out and could not see the walls or peaks of the towers as the smoke filled the district. He could feel his breathing quicken but the stench of the air became frighteningly familiar. Cassius grabbed tight to Basimick and pulled him close to whisper, "Be brave here, lad. Best be braver than ever. You are a dragon hunter and a city sheriff at that. There will be time later to worry."

Basimick looked at the short dragon hunter and tried to force his mind to understand. "What are we going to do?" His breathing was still loud but he was trying to focus on an order, a goal, or anything other than where his mind wanted to dwell.

Longinus then looked out and Basimick could tell that even the tall one was unable to control his thoughts for the moment. "There aren't any elves out," he said slowly. "We could make for the walls and see how to get out of the city from there." He took a step through the threshold of the vault and tried to guess the volley of the elves. "Arrows are becoming a bit more regular now. We could try to make for cover."

Basimick took a deep breath to settle and he stepped out of the vault. "There, the door of that tower is open. We could see further down the avenue from there."

They both looked back at Cassius but he was holding tight to the guard's axe. "You two go along and get out of here."

"Old friend," Longinus stepped back through the door and put his hand on Cassius' shoulder. He drew him in and held him tightly for a moment before stepping back to look him in the eyes again. "Always the hero."

Cassius smiled, "See something."

"Do something," Longinus nodded.

They both looked at Basimick and Cassius smiled so wide his eyes wrinkled. "If any of us get out, lad, you must."

"We can all get out," Basimick reassured himself.

Longinus looked around and could see the wounded that were left unattended as the battle outside worsened. "Who would help here," he said plainly, as though it were simply his nature to offer his assistance. "We could help them, and if you can, go get us help." The dragon hunter smiled but his eyes were giving away the truth.

Cassius stepped close to the door and said, "We will help out here as best we can, and you will go tell someone about this attack."

Basimick thought to argue, but he could not comprehend what he would need to do to help during such an invasion. He heard Cassius and that was all his mind could focus on. He needed to go and warn someone, get help, tell them what had happened. "Where must I go?"

Cassius and Longinus both smiled with relief as Basimick agreed to go through with the plan. Cassius began to say, "Armontrosia is north along the Marching Road, but the way is surely guarded by the elves."

"Imitheon is northward and westward through the grassland," Longinus thought. "But the Great Plains would be a rough crossing. Full of elves too." He frowned, "Tronia out west, but the biggest of the elven woods are between us and them."

"Southrunn is too far for help and too bureaucratic for timeliness," Cassius shook his head to ward off doubt. "Armontrosia is closest, and Imitheon is near, but either way is a dangerous crossing from here."

"If it is to be done then I shall do it," Basimick said with surety.

"You won't have long," Cassius stood up and listened for the horns.

"And you must avoid being caught," Longinus added, looking through the smoke.

"Here, take these," and Cassius gave up the Imperial writ as well as his dragon hunter's token. "This too, if it should ever matter," and Cassius handed Basimick the dwarven vault key where their cart had been kept safe in the Iron Keep.

Longinus gave up his own token inside a handshake with an attempted smile.

Cassius brought the young hunter into his arms. "I am so sorry, lad."

"No," Basimick hugged tightly back. "Thank you."

Longinus hugged them both tightly and then broke the embrace apart. "Go, young Basimick, before the way is shut for good." Basimick stepped through the door and turned back to his companions, but they waved for him to leave. There wasn't time for lengthy goodbyes, he had to take the moment to flee the safety of the bunker, and as he departed into the smoke the vault closed behind him, the mechanisms clanging as it locked tight.

Basimick wandered the narrow streets of the inner city. He had managed to avoid the raining arrows along the route away from the bunker vault and had been lucky enough to avoid the movement of the dwarven soldiers in the heavy smoke. Basimick rounded a corner and found himself on the eastern side of the wide main street that divided the city into an eastern and western half. Down the chasm between the tall buildings at the edge of the wall he could see the north gate of inner Ovelclutch. Dwarves in rust colored armor were gathered there, attempting to brace it shut with iron bars from an unseen foe. Eight strong dwarves struggled against the weight of the bars, lifting only one at a time, but each one fell into place across the gate to keep it shut.

"Prepare for the ram," an older warrior with a long beard shouted. "Hold the gate shut and mind the bend of the bars!" He pointed to a building near the gate and waved for someone inside. From within came a crowd of dwarven soldiers adorned in heavy armors and they were carrying large shields that rose from the ground to their height. "Mind the volley!" The teams of shield bearers held the great metal slabs above their heads and gathered about each other to roof their companions as the sky became filled once again with elven splinters.

Basimick tried to stay silent as he skulked closer toward the gate. He gripped the hilt of the sword at his waist and took a few deep breaths as he considered charging in to help. *And you will go get us help,* the voice of Cassius echoed in his head. The grip on his blade loosened as duty prevailed over his desire to join the dwarven ranks. He took a few more deep breaths to gather his wits before looking for a way out of the city. Basimick waited as the wind allowed another cloud of smoke to cross over the main road. The gust picked up and carried the smoke, turning it into wisps and the wide space cleared again, but Basimick was gone from the east corner.

He had a grip on the hilt of his sword as he ran so that the scabbard did not swing wildly about on his belt. He heard the dwarves raising the alarm again from the wall and he dove into an alley where a bridge between two dwellings protected him from the arrows raining down. Basimick covered his ears as the arrows struck the metal roofing surrounding him. It lasted close to forever it seemed, but when the noise finally gave up he darted from the narrow street and made his way around the city ring toward the western gate.

Basimick made a dash into the large interior street that followed the Imperial Way through the city as yet another volley began to fill the city with noise. He dove against the side of a tower where a stall had been built to serve in the street. The arrows were like a wave crashing from behind, rushing over, and then ahead. He was lucky enough to have avoided the deadly rain of arrows under a simple copper awning, now dented and twisted by the many barrages, but it proved itself useful as cover for the moment. As the arrows dwindled and another wave was being prepared he darted back onto the Imperial Way and sprinted westward.

At the edge of the inner ring was a round plaza near the western gate. It was vacant; the street at the edge of the wall was empty of soldiers who had been pulled to the defense of the northern gate which he could hear being crashed upon.

The gate was closed, immense, and he could hear the elves calling orders from the other side in a language he was unfamiliar with. *Opening this gate would not help,* he thought. Desperate to find a way out he wondered if climbing the rampart might be clever. *I could sneak into the outer ring and out of the open gates on the other side,* but he shook his head knowing that he could not sneak passed an army of elves.

He turned to consider returning to the vault and then he saw, turning away from the main road in the plaza, was another wide street built at a perfect angle toward the southern gate. There were small towers in the middle of the street, walking paths that terraced against each other, and within the complex park were stalls that hosted a full market for the use of the inner district. At the head of the market terrace, set adjacent to a large fountain, was a carriage being packed by a human woman.

She set down a heavy crate, wiped her brow with a sun worn sleeve, and waved for him to come closer. The woman grabbed up a simple staff, worn on the bottom with spans of travel, and she lifted a heavy book that was stitched with a strap at the spine which she slung over her shoulder. She smiled as he approached and despite the abandon in the city she did not seem surprised in the slightest that he was there.

"Who are you?" He asked the question hesitantly.

She shook her head, "Now is not the time for pleasantries, is it. You seek a way out of the city, yes?"

He was wary of the odd woman, but he needed a direction to escape. "I do."

With a laugh, as though she had just been proven right in a long standing argument, she began to shove the carriage which needed a heave of her shoulder as the wheel refused to budge on the cobble. As soon as it shifted there were wares of all sorts spilling to the ground and her shop clattered across the plaza into disarray. She didn't fret over the mess but remained smiling as she pointed at her feet. Beneath her was a metal covering in the street that had been forged to appear as part of the cobble and painted to match the plaza. "This is the only way out. Follow it westward."

"What is it? Sewers?"

"Elves from the woodlands don't think about sewers. It eludes them, but it will only be overlooked for so long."

Basimick smiled with new found hope and kneeled to pull the cover from the street, "Could the dwarves use it?"

She stepped on the cover and beyond the western gate they could both hear the orders for the elves to prepare another volley. "How many would agree to go with you? How many could before they are noticed? How should you supply the escape? Can they all outrun these armies?"

"No, but they need to be saved."

"Things are dark now, but they needn't be forever, young one," she leaned on her staff and looked down at him.

He stared up at her. "I suppose I must leave for myself." The air became noisy as the arrows rose upward to overcome the height of the wall.

"Not for yourself, right," She smiled and made sure to meet his eyes.

"No," the arrows were coming over the wall, each deadly tip prepared to strike them both down in the open street.

"You have duties."

"Yes."

"Then by your honor," she stepped off of the sewer cover. "Good luck on your travels, Basimick, son of Bassar, guard of Havvel." With a playful nod of her head the metal lid opened and quietly slid across the street.

"How do you-"

"Go." And he leapt into the hole with hope.

The brief light from above vanished as the sewer cover crashed shut and the hope drained from him again. "No! Come with me!"

The noise of the cover clanging into place settled after a moment. He tried to push the cover back open but it refused to budge. Then the thunderous roar of arrows striking the street deafened the sewer tunnel. As that noise passed, Basimick quickly went once more to open the cover and was afraid that the woman might be laying on top of the metal slab, stricken down for her assistance. He was relieved to find that only a few arrows were left to weigh the opening and he peered from beneath the metal plate, but the street was empty. There was no sign of the carriage, the mess, or the woman, just loose arrows strewn about without sign that anything had disturbed them.

Basimick lowered himself back into the sewer and caught his breath. He knew magic could open doors from lore that he had heard from pilgrims passing through Kurrum, *but the dwarven runes would halt any spells,* he remembered. "Blessings of Christianna," he nodded. "Angels. That's it."

He turned westward and managed through the dim of the long passage. Evenly spaced through the straight tunnel were holes to the surface and light would filter in just enough to see. Basimick hesitantly looked upward and found that they were chimneys and shoots with glowing glass prisms near the top. He did not spend long beneath it, though the dwellings above were likely abandoned from the attack.

He kept going, his nerves wrecked, but the sewer stench was enough to drive him forward. He covered his face with his new sleeve but the fresh cloth worked only so well. A long way later, through the sludge and grime built up by years of a gentle current from an unknown origin, a light at last showed the way out. It was as heavenly as starlight, and it grew in strength as he neared.

At last! His boots were covered in muck, his hands were coated in filth, but he could breathe. Before him was a wide pool, the edges of it dry, cracked, and crusty. The sewer runoff seeped out in a viscous goo into a dell where the grass grew tall and green around the large drying pit.

Basimick stepped out from the disgusting stream and crawled up the embankment. Eastward was the city of Ovelclutch, smoke rising as the elven army at last broke through the gates to ravage what remained. The sewers end was perhaps five spans away from the outer wall, lying across a bare and flat plain. The dwarves were certain to get the stinking sewer pits far away from the city and he found that he was well out of the path of the invaders. He was a great distance westward and northward from the elves' rear lines which seemed distracted by the assault toward the city.

Basimick went to the other end of the dell and climbed over the crest. Before him were the Great Plains, a vast expanse of tall grasses that moved like waves with the breeze so that it was like a gentle golden ocean all the way beyond sight to the horizon.

Go to get help, he thought. *You escaped for a reason*. He began westward, into the grasslands to follow with the sun.

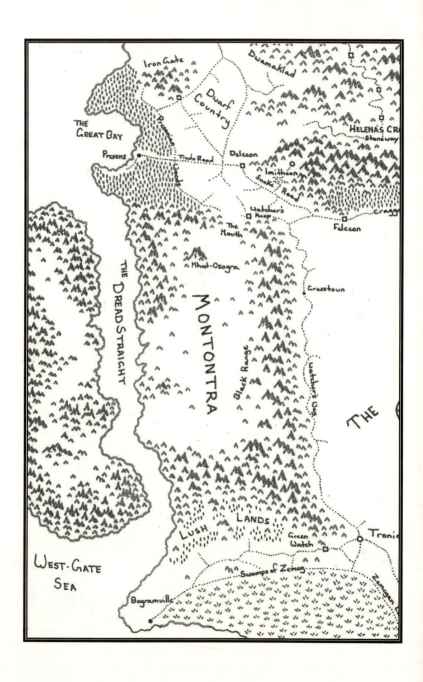

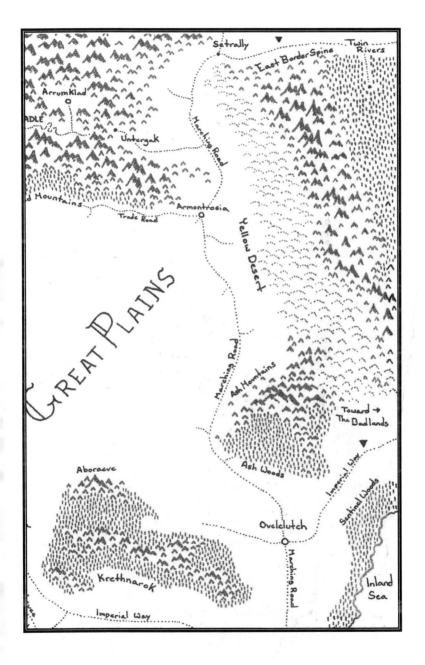

Made in the USA
Middletown, DE
17 September 2023

38596476R00137